Copyright Notice

ISBN: 978-1-953668-14-1

Author's Page

Many people have asked me, since learning I was going to release a book, 'what makes me think I can be an author?' My question, in rebuttal, is this: 'what's to make you think that you can't be an author?'

I've been writing all my life, but the fifth grade is when I developed a strong passion to write and compile short stories. I wrote so well that in the 7th grade, my teacher encouraged me to enter my story into a 'Young Authors' competition. While I didn't place first, I placed fifth out of 300 students from across the city.

My writing was the start of my show on The Heat, The Private Room. My ability to be able to speak and keep people interested quickly grew on the station and has built the fan base.

In this book, you will see quite a few references to the station, The Heat and it's one of the few references in the book that are completely real! The characters within the book are complete fiction, although many characters may display characteristics of a few people I know.

Please let me know what you all think of this work, as this is only the beginning of my writing career! Remember; don't let anyone tell you what you can't do! Do you, because only you can do you the way that you do, you...

Dedication

I would like to start by thanking all of the people who have always supported me in my journey with writing. This will include, but is not limited to, my family, my elementary school teachers, and a few of my friends!

This book is a dedication to all of my friends and family, whether they've seen my writing before or not, and I definitely cannot forget to thank you, my fan; I would not be who I am without your support!

As you read this book, I ask that you read it, as though you've never known who Ricky Ramón is; as though you've never heard my voice before; as though you've never listened to my show and have NO IDEA how I think. Read it with a new mind; if you don't know who I am, that's even better! All I ask is that you learn more about me by listening to my show on WWMR-DB: The Heat, https://theheatdb.com, and following my Facebook page (facebook.com/officialbmgage) and my Twitter (twitter.com/officialbmgage).

Last but not least, I would like to thank God for blessing me with the skills to write this book, and allowing my online radio station, WWMR-DB: The Heat, to stay on the air for 5 years and to continue to go strong!

1

The sun was shining and the air was clear as Madison and I joked on the porch of our home. I was on call for the day, so I wasn't sure if I would be called into work, but just in case, I always kept the necessities in my vehicle, such as my badge, my gun, and my handcuffs.

I increased the volume on my radio.

"And now we got the latest hit. It's called *Trust None* by Kai G, right here on Double X-L. Check it out," the personality stated before going off the air and starting the music.

"I love this dude right here. Straight from Chicago and all of the artists want to work with him," I spoke.

"Have you ever met him?" Madison asked.

"Unfortunately, no," I shook my head, "but it's on my to-do list. I've spoken with some of his artists, including Ari Love, but never to him. Dude is hard to get in touch with," I joked.

"Well," Madison spoke, "you'll team up with him eventually," she kissed my cheek. "Everyone who's anyone knows that you're the big boss."

"And don't you ever forget it," I laughed.

As I finished my statement, the police radio sounded.

"Dispatch to Young, come in Young," the dispatcher spoke.

"Young, here," I responded into the receiver.

"Please go to your reporting station for an emergency meeting. Your presence is required."

This was anticipated, even though I wasn't scheduled. I was one to jump at the opportunity to help my city, even though the city's current relationship with the police wasn't the best.

"10-4" I responded to the dispatcher.

"I guess you better get on down there," Madison joked. "Don't worry about me, I'll hold it down," she laughed.

"Alright, baby," I gave her a hug and a kiss. "I'll be back soon."

I drove until I arrived at the station. I exited my vehicle and entered the front of the building.

"Isabella, what's good?" I laughed.

She jokingly rolled her eyes and chuckled.

"All I know is that you better get your ass in that meeting before Abel chops your *cojones* off," she joked.

"Damn, it's like that," I spoke as she directed me to the room.

I looked on her desk, reached over, and grabbed the piece of candy from her cup.

"I'm taking this with me," I put it in my pocket.

She scoffed, shook her head, and smiled.

I quietly entered the room and found many officers listening to Abel. Some were in uniform, others were in plain clothes.

I found an empty seat next to Tim, a fellow officer.

"What's up?" I whispered.

"Not much at all," he responded. "He's just getting started. Something about Linda and Julie, I hear."

"Well, let's see," I replied.

I checked my phone for any notifications and put it in my pocket.

Abel proceeded to speak.

"As you know, crime has recently been on the rise. That crime has been affecting not only the citizens of the city but also our own department," he cleared his throat.

"Yea, and the fact that the city has a bad rapport with the police right now, it's not going to get any better," I mumbled under my breath.

"Over the past year, we have had over 75 officers shot and wounded and 150 that have been murdered. Those officers that were critically wounded and murdered were due to violence in the city and our bad rep. We have to find a way to increase positivity and change the views of Chicago PD."

Abel pressed a button on the remote that switched slides on the projector.

"Now, just a few months ago, Young received a promotion because of the difference he's making and the heights he's willing to go to help his team," he pressed the button and my image appeared on the screen as well as some of my statistics.

"Alone, in the past year, he has made two hundred arrests and has been able to de-escalate at least a hundred situations. Let's add that he's only had to fire his weapon seven times last year."

My fellow police officers applauded me and I looked around and nodded.

I didn't like to have the spotlight. My job wasn't about me. I was doing what I loved to help my city and better the community, not for bragging rights.

"Since he's so strong in the force, we're going to move a few things around. Young," he spoke to me directly, "you will temporarily be partnering up with Officer Charles," he looked at Tim. "Since he's one of our rookies, I take it that you'll show him the ropes."

"Roberts, Officer Hubbard is my partner," I rose to my feet. "We've been keeping things clean around here, so I don't think we should just switch things up."

"Yeah, I mean, no offense, Cap, but if it's not broken, don't fix it," Jared spoke.

"We're trying some new things out," Abel spoke. "We're going to add 'flying' to your abilities, so we want for you to be able to attack this with a fresh mind. And while you're picking up on your skill, you can show Officer Charles the ropes," he reiterated.

I sat down and I continued.

"Unfortunately, I don't know how to fly," I chuckled.

"No problem. We got a deal worked out with the aviation school to assist you. And the helicopters that we have, they're going to be fully equipped with navigation via longitude and latitude. It also has a training mode, where the system actually helps you fly. But note, during assignments, this mode will not work, so you better practice," he added.

"I guess you've thought all of this out, huh?" I asked.

"Always on top of the game," Abel added as he switched slides. "Now, on to a different subject; you all may or may not have heard, but Linda Jackson was released from prison yesterday."

Hearing about Linda made my body shiver. Ever since she betrayed the force, she lost all of my respect.

"Julie Wilson is also getting released tomorrow; both for good behavior," Abel added.

"Are you kidding me?" I mumbled.

"And as they say, what doesn't kill you will only make you stronger."

"So, the fact that they didn't serve the full terms in jail and are being put back out on the streets, they may have gotten smarter on the inside, and need to be watched," I announced to the other officers.

"Exactly!"Abel stated.

"So, how do you want us to go about this?" Tim asked as he took notes.

"Well, you and Detective Young will be in charge of this. I want for you to watch him and follow his lead."

Abel slid a piece of paper down the table to me.

"Young, this is the address to the airport that all of the helicopters are kept. This is your helicopter number, as well as the pad number you are allotted."

"How much does it cost to manage a helicopter?" I asked.

"Nothing at all, to you. It is coming out of the department's funds."

"I suppose I could try something new," I stated.

"Great news, although it's not like you had a choice," Abel lightly laughed. "And the rest of you all just keep your eyes peeled," he stated.

I left the meeting and walked towards the exit of the police building.

"Got your ass chewed out enough?" Isabella asked.

"Better," I started. "Guess who's on aerial support."

Isabella closed the folder she was holding.

"Congratulations. I guess you're getting bonuses left and right."

"Yea, but they can keep this bonus," I joked.

I exited the station and walked to where my vehicle used to be parked, but to my surprise, all of the cars were moved from the lot and onto the street, except for my vehicle.

A helicopter sat in the lot, and I knew that had to be for me.

"Where's my car?" I asked the pilot as I opened the door to the helicopter.

"It's been towed to the airport; no charge," he shouted over the propellers. "Get in," the pilot told me as he exited the aircraft.

"What are you doing?" I asked him as he walked around to my side.

"Well you're flying us back," he told me.

"I don't know how to fly," I stated as I walked around to the pilot's seat of the helicopter.

"That's why I am here, to make sure you understand. Here take these."

He handed me a headset with a microphone connected.

"And this is for?" I asked.

"For communicating with the control tower and your co-pilot."

I got in the pilot's seat and I was looking for the seatbelt, expecting it to be the same as a car. The pilot showed me the seatbelt and ensured it was tight around me.

The pilot entered a code into the control panel and the helicopter emitted a chime to notify us that it was in practice mode.

The helicopter's computer started to read off directions. It told me how to enter where I was going and referred me to the radar; the more it beeped, the closer I was. It then told me to start the engine. I started the engine and the propellers began to rotate. The helicopter instructed me to raise the lever. I raised the lever and the helicopter started to levitate and I shook a little.

"Where are we going to land this?" I questioned.

"We are flying to the airport to land the helicopter," the trainer spoke. "Now you have lifted the lever, keep your hands on this," he referred to an object that I assumed was the steering device.

I grabbed it and waited. When the helicopter was high enough, the pilot instructed me to accelerate and steer to the left. He also told me that the radar would also tell me if I was approaching another plane or helicopter.

The radar was already set for the airport's latitude and longitude, so it was directing me to the airport with a series of beeps; the closer I was to the destination, the faster it would beep, and the beeps would be slower the further away I was,

Minutes had passed, but it seemed like hours, and now it was time to land the helicopter.

"First, you want to pull down on the lever," the pilot told me, "but keep accelerating, or else the chopper will descend at a rapid rate."

I lowered the lever and slowly I felt the engine halt.

"Now, make sure you are right above the landing pad."

I hovered over the landing pad and held the helicopter steady.

"Slowly release the accelerator," he instructed over his headset to me.

I followed his instruction and the helicopter lowered slowly onto the launch pad.

The pilot got out first, walked over to my side of the helicopter, helped me properly turn the engine off, and lock the helicopter onto the landing pad.

"Here are the keys to the helicopter and now it's yours," he replied to me.

"You sure you want to part with this beauty?" I asked him sarcastically.

"Thanks, but no thanks. It's all yours," he chuckled. "I'm going to step inside and wait for my ride."

I shook hands with the pilot and he walked inside of the building.

I located my car in the parking lot and climbed inside. I started the engine, looked at the helicopter one final time, and drove away.

2

"You've been gone a long time," Madison greeted me.

"I'm just coming from the airport," I told her shaking my head. "I had to land the helicopter and drive back home."

"And why do you have a helicopter?" she asked.

"Abel assigned it to me. I am officially on aerial support and ground duty."

"So, what? You're going to be away from home now or something," she chuckled.

"You mean more than before?" I laughed.

"Young and Charles, Linda and Julie are both on the move. We just want to keep an eye out for anything suspicious on their part," Abel spoke over the radio.

"I thought Julie was being released tomorrow," I inquisitively rubbed my 5 o'clock shadow.

"She was supposed to be released tomorrow, but the system decided to release her and Linda today. Not my choice," he responded.

"10-4. Where are they?"

"They are about to enter Wisconsin. You won't catch up to them by ground, so please resort to being airborne."

"Officer Charles, please report to the airport," I instructed and turned down my radio.

"Madison, I would take you with me, but this is police business. I'm not sure how Abel would respond to you being in the helicopter with me if something were to go down, without having a dated waiver," I chuckled.

"A waiver for what?" she asked.

"In case you were to take a bullet, you wanted to eat a bullet, or in case you were to get injured, the waiver would state that you understand the dangers of tagging along and you won't sue the broke-ass city," I laughed.

"Well, I'm not signing that right now," Madison chuckled as she kissed me.

"I'll be back, baby," I spoke as I got into my vehicle and drove away.

The drive to the airport was silent; I didn't want any distractions; I had to focus on the upcoming flight.

I was almost at the airport when my cellphone rang. I answered on the first ring.

"Richard, I know you're probably freaking out," Abel chuckled, "so I got a co-pilot to fly with you on these first few rounds."

Hearing this lifted a bunch of stress from my shoulders.

"That's exactly what I needed to hear," I replied.

Abel laughed.

"I thought you'd like to hear it. He should be waiting for you when you get to the airport and is going to assist you during these flights; at least until you and Tim are trained properly on how to fly and maintain the aircraft."

"I'm pulling into the airport now. I'm going to keep you informed as to what's going on," I replied.

"10-4. Talk to you soon," Abel ended the call.

I parked my vehicle and walked inside the airport. I saw Tim and the co-pilot standing next to him.

"You must be Richard. I'm Cameron Little, your co-pilot," he spoke. "You set?" he asked me as we shook hands.

"Nice to meet you, Cameron. Let's go," I replied.

We left the building and walked over to the helicopter.

"You sure you're jazzy enough?" I joked with Tim about his attire.

Tim wore a shirt and tie and dress pants; it looked like he had on a tuxedo, but without the jacket.

"Man, you're just mad you don't look this good even on your best days."

"Yeah, I'm going to let you keep on dreaming," I spoke as I unlocked the helicopter.

I got in the pilot's seat and Cameron got into the co-pilot's seat. Tim sat in the back.

"Y'all set?" I asked as I started the aircraft.

"Take off," Tim chuckled.

"Young to Roberts," I spoke over the headset as I levitated.

Cameron adjusted his headset and flipped switches on the aircraft.

"Go ahead," Abel replied.

"What kind of vehicle are we looking for?" I asked as the helicopter flew North.

"Red Chevy Impala; license plate Umbrella-Robert-Frank-William-Daniel -2-6"

"We'll keep watch. We're about 10 minutes out from Wisconsin."

"So much quicker than driving," Tim chuckled. "It would take us at least an hour and a half if we decided to drive."

"Yea, but when you're pushing 500 and you don't have to worry about traffic, you're in pretty decent condition," Cameron laughed. "Richard, press that button right there," he directed my attention to a switch that was illuminated.

I flipped the switch and the monitor turned on, which was connected to the helicopter's camera.

"Oh damn," I spoke in awe. "Hella convenient. You see them?" I asked as we flew over vehicles.

"Yeah, there they are," Tim spoke as he looked through the binoculars.

Cameron spotted the vehicle on the monitor and tapped the screen to lock the video on the car.

He zoomed in and I saw two figures sitting in the front seat.

"When you need to, press this button to focus the camera and get a clear view of the subject. The camera also has facial recognition which is linked to CPD's database," he tapped an icon on the screen, and light was applied to the figures.

The screen scanned and cleared the image.

Julie was driving and Linda was sitting in the passenger's seat.

"They're just laughing it up, huh?" I chuckled. "They have no idea," I shook my head.

Cameron flipped a few more switches to stabilize the helicopter and control the engine.

A transmission came through the radio as I watched Julie pull into a gas station. She pulled out her phone.

"Dispatch to all available units. We have a 34s at the Hancock building. Suspects are reported to be armed and dangerous. No visual description of the potential suspects, so take advanced precautions in apprehending."

I knew the call was for all available officers.

"This is shield 4352 responding to the 34s. En route to the location," I responded to the dispatcher. "Roberts, should I go by car or use the chopper?" I radioed Abel as Cameron flipped a few switches to turn to reverse the engine.

"Use the bird and go retrieve members of the SWAT team. Once you get to the Hancock building, there will be a licensed officer directing you to the landing zone. I'm sending the latitude and longitude to your GPS now."

"10-4," I returned the receiver to the dashboard.

"CPD doesn't play, huh?" Cameron asked. "It's your first time flying, but when they call, you gotta go.

"That's the way it is," I chuckled.

"Did you ever think about just throwing in the towel?" he asked as he put on the bullet-proof vest that resided under his chair.

"I mean, it has its days," I slightly shrugged. "But I enjoy what I do."

"Are you forgetting we have a job to do?" Tim interrupted.

"Shut up Tim, before I throw you out this helicopter," I told him with a chuckle.

Cameron turned off the facial recognition, so that the camera's view wouldn't stay locked on Linda and Julie, and adjusted his headset.

"Let's turn this bird around," Cameron spoke.

I moved the control to the left and held it in one position. The helicopter turned around slowly, and Cameron flipped more switches to restart the engine.

I continued the flight to the Hancock building.

While flying, I heard numerous transmissions regarding the shooting. Some transmissions were to alert which officers were replying to the situation, some were providing instructions, while others were from officers at the scene of the crime, providing updates.

I decided to pick up my phone and call Jared. I wasn't sure if he'd received the transmission, but I would feel more comfortable knowing he was by my side.

"Speak on it," he stated.

"Jared, it's me, Richard," I replied.

"What's up, man?" he asked me.

"On duty. Meet me on the top of the building with latitude and longitude of -42.045275, -88.291684. We have to take this case. There's a shooting at the Hancock building."

"Do I look like I read latitude and longitude?" Jared replied with a chuckle.

"Man, you better put your police skills to work," I chuckled. "Roberts has me flying there to retrieve the SWAT team."

"Bet," Jared hung up the phone.

Within a matter of minutes, I was approaching the building and I saw an officer with neon lights, waving them to alert me where to land.

"We've been cleared to land," Cameron spoke. "Don't kill the engine this time, just flip this switch and decelerate," he pointed to the switch that I should flip.

I flipped the switch and decelerated. The propellers continued to rotate as the helicopter lowered.

The SWAT team loaded the helicopter with weapons and ammunition. They gave Tim, Cameron, Jared, and me bulletproof vests.

I returned to the pilot's seat of the helicopter as Jared and the rest of the SWAT team got inside. While I was in the air, the SWAT team was loading the guns and aiming them out the side of the helicopter.

"Young, are you en route?" Abel asked over my headset.

"In route to the Hancock building," I replied.

"10-4."

I arrived over the ground and decided to fly over the building. Another officer, also with neon lights, waved them around for the helicopter to land. Because there wasn't a landing pad, it was up to the designated officers to direct where the helicopter could land.

I landed the helicopter and the SWAT team, in almost an instant, all unloaded.

Cameron was the first to exit, Tim got out next and Jared followed. I was the last to exit the aircraft.

We ran down the stairs, each of us holding guns. We snuck around the back, where we saw the SWAT team aiming their guns at someone.

"Chicago P-D! Get on the ground, now!" I shouted to the fugitive.

The suspect turned around and looked at me.

Without hesitation, they pivoted their head and spoke into their right shoulder.

I was unable to hear what they said, but once they spoke, hundreds of people started to evacuate the building with guns. Trucks and cars exited the parking garage.

The police fired at the suspect, but the suspect ducked and got out amid the confusion.

The SWAT team opened fire at the new shooters; some bullets hit, others missed. The fugitives were shooting at the police and bullets hit various members of the force, including Tim, Abel, and other units.

I didn't take my focus from wanting to catch the primary suspect.

I took cover as I ran over to the entrance of the building.

Jared was shooting wildly; clip after clip, he was shooting at the suspects.

I ran inside the building with some other members of the SWAT team, to potentially find the suspect in charge of the operation.

One door was unlocked and one of the officers pushed it open. We all ran inside, guns aimed; we started to look everywhere and I discovered a beeping noise.

"You all hear that?" I asked and silenced the rest of the team.

"Sounds like a bomb," one of the officers replied.

I searched the area and found a timer counting down.

"We have six minutes to either clear this entire area or to disarm the bomb."

I heard additional helicopters arriving on the scene. I looked out of the window of the building and saw that news helicopters were broadcasting what was going on back to their respective news outlets.

"I'm going to leave you all up here to try to disarm the bomb," I spoke to the team. "I'm going back down and get rid of those helicopters. I need a sniper rifle," I uttered.

One of the officers handed me a sniper rifle and I ran downstairs. When I got downstairs, I managed to tune into the helicopters' frequency on my radio.

"Get these choppers outta here," I stated.

There was no response from the pilots nor the copilots.

I aimed my sniper rifle at the helicopter and I fired a bullet at the camera. "Leave!" I shouted again, "unless, you other choppers want your equipment damaged. The next shots will not just be for equipment," I yelled.

The helicopters started to vanish and I jogged over to Abel.

As the helicopters disappeared, so did many of the suspects.

"Roberts, are you okay?" I asked him.

I could see he was shot in his shoulder.

"Young, I need to get to a hospital soon. I'm losing too much blood too quickly. Get me a chopper," he uttered.

His radio was destroyed.

"Can I just fly you to the hospital?" I kneeled to him.

"That's not what you are for. You are not a medical chopper, so you cannot land near a hospital. Or you could get our whole department in trouble," Abel stated to me.

"Officer down; can we get a medical chopper to the Hancock building?" I stated over my radio.

"10-4; we have an officer down at the Hancock building. Requesting chopper," the dispatch spoke over the radio.

I walked back over to Abel and spoke to him.

"What do you want me to do?"

As I asked the question, several SWAT team members ran outside.

"We can't disarm the bomb. It is rigged so that if we even attempt to diffuse it, it will blow," one of the members told me.

Suddenly, the cars that remained inside of the lot started to disappear into the streets.

"Damn it," I yelled.

"The entire building has been evacuated," he assured me.

I looked up and I saw the helicopter for Abel above. The aircraft started to lower and I lifted him into the helicopter.

The helicopter levitated and flew away. I called for Jared and Cameron on the radio to meet me atop the building before running to the stairs.

Once I reached the top of the building, I put my weapon in the aircraft.

Jared and the rest of the SWAT team came up the stairs.

"Let's go," I spoke aloud.

The SWAT members loaded their weapons into the vehicle and proceeded to climb inside. Jared got into the aircraft following the SWAT team. Cameron proceeded to get into the co-pilot's seat.

"Where's Officer Charles?" Jared asked.

"Officer Young to Charles. Come in, Charles," I spoke over the radio.

There was no response from him so I tried again a few seconds later.

"Charles, please report with your location."

Again, no response.

"Not sure," I spoke to Jared, "but we gotta get the hell out of here."

I started the helicopter and it levitated. Cameron flipped switches as the helicopter levitated and kept an eye on the altimeter.

Once we reached our desired altitude, I flew the helicopter forward. Another transmission came through.

"Aerial unit, keep eyes on the suspect. Red Nissan Skyline, no plates, front bumper damage. Traveling westbound on the Stevenson."

"10-4," I replied over the headset.

Cameron watched the helicopter's camera and turned on the night vision for a clearer view.

Blockades were set to prevent cars from proceeding onto the expressway; we didn't want to jeopardize anyone for this suspect's erratic driving.

"There it is," Cameron spoke as he locked the view of the camera on the car.

Cameron flipped a switch to stall the engine of the helicopter to allow me to decrease altitude.

I flew over the vehicle and further decreased the helicopter's altitude since I knew we would have to stall the car's engine in some fashion.

Multiple police officers were also chasing the suspect; as a result, rather than hovering over the suspect, I flew in front of the vehicle.

Since Jared was by a door, he aimed his AK-47 at the grill of the vehicle.

The vehicle came to a hard decrease in speed.

"Get the grill," I spoke over the headset and Jared began shooting at the grill of the car.

The suspect stepped on the brakes once again and turned their wheels to the right.

Once the car turned to the right, Jared stopped firing the weapon, as he didn't want to hit the suspect. The car halted completely.

"Detective Young, lowering the chopper and taking the lead," I spoke over the headset as I completely lowered the helicopter. "Stay alert with guns aimed and ready," I spoke to Cameron and the SWAT team.

I opened the door to the helicopter and drew my gun from the holster.

Multiple officers also emerged from their vehicles and surrounded the suspect.

I walked closer with my gun aimed.

I quickly opened the door and the suspect put her hands up. I looked and noticed a picture of Julie in her windshield.

3

I lowered my gun and the other officers pulled her out of the car.

"Hold on, guys," I replied. "I got this."

Seeing the picture of Julie in the windshield opened the door to all kinds of questions.

The fact that Julie was released from prison today, and this occurred, was no coincidence.

The other officers released her and I held her arm.

I walked her over to the helicopter. Although I knew I couldn't fly her back to the station, I wanted to get a head start and identify who I would be interrogating once I got back.

"I don't know anything," she started.

"I haven't even asked you anything, yet," I spoke to her. "Look, I'm not here to play games. I don't know who you are or why you just did what you did; you're the only one who knows and can provide some level of insight."

The woman was silent and looked around as if she were looking for an escape.

"Ma'am, do you see those officers back there? They truly don't give a care what happens to you," I started. "But me, you're lucky that I brought you to the side."

"And why do you care?" she asked.

"I'm going to be honest with you," I began. "When I opened that car door, you surrendered, but I also saw a picture of a woman in your dashboard: Julie Wilson. Now, if you help me, I help you," I explained to her.

"Yeah, right, like I'm supposed to believe you right now when there are officers just waiting to shoot me down like a dog."

"I'm your best bet right now," I retaliated. "I'm trying to help you out."

Jared exited the helicopter with his pistol in hand.

"Best bet, my ass," she spoke.

She was getting nervous when she saw Jared come around with his weapon in hand. "*¿Sabes que?* Just do whatever you're going to do."

Jared chuckled.

"My partner is trying to help you, and you're being stubborn as if you aren't interested in his assistance."

"Can't save someone who doesn't want to be saved," I replied.

The suspect decided to speak.

"My name is Jamie Perez. Julie Wilson is my aunt," she confessed.

"Your aunt?" I asked, inquisitively.

"Yes," she replied.

I looked to the right and saw that the officers still had their guns raised.

I raised my badge to alert them to lower their weapons.

"This is what we're going to do," I started. "I'm going to escort you back over to my team and they're going to place you under arrest. They're going to drive you back to the station and I am going to meet you there for questioning. When I arrive, I want for you to tell me the whole story," I spoke.

"Yes, sir," she replied.

Jared patted my shoulder as I walked her back over to the rest of the officers.

"You all take her back to the station. I'll be there in a few moments for questioning. Mirandize her and everything, but do not process her into the system," I spoke to the lady officer who took hold of Jamie's arm.

"Yes, sir," she replied as she walked away. "Do you have any weapons on you?" she asked Jamie.

"Any motives?" Jared asked as he stood at my side.

"No information yet. I'm going to meet them back at the station for questioning. But get this," I started.

"What's up?" Jared asked.

"Julie Wilson is her aunt," I replied as I walked back to the helicopter.

"Think that shit is a coincidence?" Jared asked.

"I think not," I answered.

Jared and I got back into the helicopter before I spoke again.

"We're going to fly back to the airport," I announced to the team. "Let's request a car be there to pick you all up."

"Sounds good," one of the members spoke.

"Let's get this baby off the ground," Cameron spoke. "I'm going to let you take this lead this time," he said to me.

***

"So, what is this about Julie Wilson?" I asked Jamie as I arrived back at the station.

Jamie was nervous. I could tell this was the first time she'd ever been arrested or questioned by the police.

Her eyes became engorged with tears.

Jared brought a box of Kleenex over to her and she took one from the box.

"Take your time," I uttered softly to her.

"But not too much time," Jared spoke. "We need some answers sooner than later."

I could tell that Jared was making her uncomfortable.

"Jared, step out for a moment," I mentioned.

"You want me to leave you in here with this criminal?" he chuckled. "That's not going to happen."

"I got this," I replied with a serious tone.

He sighed.

"It's your call," Jared stated before exiting the room.

"Now, Jamie, I want to help you. But I can't help you unless you help me," I said to her. "Tell me about what went down and what the deal is with Julie."

Jamie wiped her tears using a Kleenex.

"How old are you, Jamie?" I asked.

"I'm 25."

"Do you work?" I interrogated.

"No," she responded.

"So, what do you do?"

"I'm a student," she answered as she adjusted her hair from her face.

"How do you get money to support yourself and schooling?"

"Truth be told, my aunt usually helps me with all of that. But her assets and bank accounts were frozen once she went to prison, so these past few years have been rough for me," Jamie sniffled. "So, I've been just helping out in different places for money."

"Well, for one, it's a good thing that the assets were frozen because if you'd have touched them, things wouldn't have been too bright for you. You would have been imprisoned along with your aunt."

Jamie's cheeks turned pink.

"And two, I understand that things are rough, but how does that put us where we are today?"

"Uh..." she started.

"Jamie, you've got to tell me the truth. It's the only way I can help you," I calmly told her.

"Officer," she hesitated.

"Detective," I corrected.

"I can't tell you."

"Look," I spoke, "I can't help you at all if you don't tell me something. Here's a list of laws that you broke today," I spoke as I passed her a notepad. "Attempted murder of police officers, felony evading, speeding, terrorism, vandalism; the list goes on and on, Jamie," I finished.

Tears began to run down her cheeks as she listened and reviewed the list.

"And I don't think this orange jumpsuit would do you justice, Ms. Lady," I chuckled.

Jamie continued to look at the pad and sighed.

"Did your aunt have anything to do with what just occurred?" I asked the question that was beating at my chest this entire time.

"Yes," Jamie hesitantly admitted.

"Tell me what happened, Jamie," I replied.

Jamie looked around, nervously, before speaking.

"My aunt came over to my house, just moments after she was released. I guess I was her first point-of-contact," Jamie nervously chuckled as she fidgeted her hands together. "I was so excited to see my aunt, I mean after all it had been a year."

I wrote down the details of what Jamie was telling me as she explained.

"She handed me $500 in cash and told me all about her experiences in jail; how she had horrible in-mates and everything. She then told me that she had a job for me to do, but it was risky as hell. She said that she had a bunch of people waiting to do a drop for her at the Hancock building and she needed my help."

"So, this is how it all began?" I uttered.

"Yes," Jamie replied and continued. "My aunt then went into specifics on how I should execute the job."

"I'm going to need details on what she told you to do," I explained to Jamie.

She sighed another sigh. I could tell she was nervous.

"She said it was supposed to be a simple operation on my part. The objective was to be in and be out in under ten minutes. I was supposed to start a commotion, let the cops show up, and then run around back and escape in my little red corvette," Jamie chuckled but tears flowed down her face.

But you're in a Skyline.

"That doesn't sound like much of a drop," I spoke.

"The objective was to destroy evidence that was gathered against her and she knew some officers would be caught up in it; she mentioned you in particular, Detective," Jamie explained.

Wow, Julie really has it out for me.

"She explained that someone would bring me a package that I would have to destroy. She said it had evidence against the entire family, and if it wasn't discarded correctly, we could all go down. The package was doused in gasoline and given to me; I had to burn it somehow. So, what I did, I shot the package with the pistol she gave me. If all went well, she was supposed to give me another $5000."

Jamie continued to fidget with her fingers.

She used another Kleenex to dry her eyes.

"I'll be right back, Jamie," I told her before walking out of the room.

"What are you thinking?" Jared asked as I closed the door to the interrogation room.

"I think she's being honest," I shrugged my shoulders. "But I still think that she's holding back. I gotta find a way to make her crack." I told Jared.

"I don't think she did that shit for the money," Jared admitted.

"You don't?" I asked him.

"Nah," Jared slightly shook his head. "It's something deeper than that. That girl is truly scared," he spoke.

"Whatever it is, we're about to get to the bottom of this," I replied before giving him our signature handshake.

I re-entered the room and sat down.

"Jamie, I know it wasn't for the money. Why did you really do it?" I jumped straight into the question.

"You wouldn't understand," she told me with her head down.

I thought for a moment and thought about Julie's antics and how she performed.

"Did Julie threaten you?" I quietly asked.

Jamie teared up.

"Talk to me," I urged her for an answer.

"Yes," she finally whispered.

"What did she threaten to do?" I asked Jamie.

"You ever been threatened to do something by your own family member, who has been known to snap at any given notice?" Jamie shook her head.

"I can't say that I have," I spoke.

"I was promised a hospital bed if I didn't pull off the job and I was promised death if I were to get caught and tell the police," Jamie started to look around as if Julie was somewhere nearby.

"Look at me," I told Jamie as I began to feel sympathetic towards her. "She will not hurt you," I told her.

"Thank you," Jamie whispered to me.

She leaned in for a hug.

I allowed her to hug me and proceeded to talk.

"Jamie, if what you're telling me is true, that means that your aunt is going to strike again, and she isn't done with her old ways," I started. "Work with me, and I'm sure we can arrange to keep you out of prison, put your aunt back where she belongs, and keep you safe," I rose to my feet. "You will stay here in a cell overnight and I'll let you know exactly what's going to happen tomorrow," I informed her.

"Thank you," Jamie replied as she rose to her feet.

I tapped on the glass and an officer walked in.

"No cuffs," I instructed. "Just put her in her own holding cell," I instructed.

"No problem," the officer spoke as he escorted Jamie from the room.

I exited the room and didn't see Jared, so I proceeded to the front desk to alert Isabella about what was occurring with Jamie.

I didn't want to risk anything happening to our potential star suspect-slash-witness.

4

The next day, I drove until I reached the hospital they had flown Abel to.

I walked inside with my gun on my side and approached the front desk.

"Abel Roberts, please?" I asked.

"Your name?" the secretary asked me.

"Richard Young, part of his CPD unit." I showed her my badge.

"Straight to the back, through those double doors. Once you see the news-stand, make a right. You'll know his room when you see it," she told me.

"Thank you," I told her and I proceeded towards his room.

I walked through the double doors and followed the receptionists' directions to get to his room. I saw two men standing outside of a door, and I knew right away that the room belonged to Abel.

Two muscular police officers stood in front of the door. The men resembled bodyguards guarding a celebrity's room.

I showed them my badge and they let me proceed into the room.

"Knock, knock," I stated as I walked into the room. "Roberts?"

"Over here, Young," Abel responded.

I walked over to find him lying in bed. His arm was elevated by a sling.

"How are you doing?" I asked him as I sat down in the chair.

"A lot better. They got me to the ER just in time," he mentioned. "Did you catch the suspect?" he asked.

"Yea, I caught her," I started; Abel interrupted me.

"Her?"

"Yea," I started. "And guess who she's related to."

"Who?" he chuckled.

"Our star criminal, Julie Wilson," I announced with a chuckle. "She blamed Julie for what recently went down."

Abel displayed a confused expression.

"Do you think she's being honest?" he asked me.

"There's only one way to find out. I'm requesting permission to head over to her residence."

"Whose residence? Julie's?"

"Yes," I answered.

"No, no, no, no, no," he began as he pressed the button to raise the head of the bed. "She's fresh out of jail, and we can't have you all going over and spooking her because of what a suspect has accused," Abel explained.

"Roberts, we have good intel that this could be Julie's work," I reasoned. "Julie has always been a master at planning and executing; who's to say she couldn't orchestrate this from inside a cell?"

"Young, I can't allow the force to have a case lingering over its head," he explained.

"Jared and I will investigate this, low-key," I explained. "You won't even know we're working the case." I was adamant to get to the bottom of this.

He sighed and continued, "You really think she's responsible for this even though she just got out?" he asked.

"All I'm saying is that I wouldn't put this shit past her," I spoke. "Jared and I will just go by her house and talk to her; nothing major."

Abel thought for a moment before speaking.

"I'm going to let you all work this, but if something goes sour," he began.

"I'm already knowing," I replied with a laugh.

"Have you heard from Tim?" Abel asked me as he changed subjects.

"I haven't heard from him since the incident that went down yesterday," I shook my head. "I hate to say it, but I think Tim may be dead."

"That's not the case," Abel chuckled. "I just spoke with him. Apparently, he was able to get airlifted to a hospital. I need for someone to explain how he got airlifted with no radio communication," Abel laughed.

"Better ask him, since he's alive," I joked. "Only he can answer that question," I impersonated 'Smokey the Bear'.

Abel laughed at my impersonation and looked at the clock on the wall.

"Sounds to me like you better tuck ass and get out of here," he mentioned.

"I'll call you in a bit to check on everything, Roberts," I replied before leaving the room.

I exited the hospital with one thing on my mind: Julie.

I wanted to get to the bottom of this case before it truly got started and the only lead I had was a suspect in jail, who claimed to be Julie's niece, and that she was responsible for everything that happened.

I had a choice to make: either I believe Jamie or I believe a criminal who had me running in circles for years.

Jamie, it was.

I got in my vehicle and called Jared.

"Speak on it," he answered.

"We got a job to do, sweetheart," I laughed. "Be at my place in about 20 minutes. We're gonna go talk to Ms. Wilson."

"Who? Jamie?" Jared asked. "I thought she had a different last name."

"Nah, the mastermind," I started. "Julie."

***

I drove until I arrived at Julie's house.

"You all set?" I asked Jared.

"Let's do this shit," he replied as he unbuckled his seatbelt.

Jared made sure his gun was secure in his holster as I knocked on the door.

"Who is it?" Julie asked through the door.

"It's Detective Young, Julie," I stated.

She slowly opened the door.

"If you're here about a bank robbery, I didn't do it," she chuckled. "I'm keeping clean this time around," she spoke.

"Luckily for you, we're not here about any robbery," I emitted a small laugh.

"She's got jokes," Jared uttered.

"I'm only kidding," she spoke. "Please, come on inside."

Jared and I walked inside of her home and sat down on the couch she pointed to.

"Would you all care for a cup of tea? Water? Anything?" Julie asked us.

"No, Julie, we're good," I answered.

"So, what brings you all here today?" she asked me.

I noticed that she never sat down.

"Well, we heard you were released from jail, and just wanted to make sure everything was alright," I answered.

"Is this a regular thing? To follow up with ex-cons?" Julie asked.

"We like to keep our unit on top," I spoke. "We like to check up on our ex-criminals to make sure they're doing alright, especially those who are bright and have great potential," I subtly hinted.

"How are you holding up?" Jared asked.

"I'm just trying to get reacquainted with being a free woman," Julie emitted a nervous chuckle.

"You'll be reacquainted in no time," Jared replied.

I visually scanned Julie's home as she and Jared spoke. I saw nothing suspicious from where I sat, but I still didn't want to put this past her. Still, I didn't want to spook her without having some kind of break in the case.

I pretended to answer my phone as if a call came through.

I excused myself from Jared and Julie and walked towards the door.

I touch my slight stubble of a beard and hung up moments later.

"Jared, we gotta get going," I interrupted. "Got some things we have to take care of," I lied.

"Alright, cool," Jared rose to his feet. "Julie, it's great to see that you're doing well, and hopefully our next encounter will be similar to this one," he laughed. "Nice and calm and friendly."

Julie chuckled.

"Well, I thank you all for stopping by," Julie responded, "and hopefully our next encounter is one like this. Don't stay away for long," she enunciated as we walked to the car.

"Well, she seems like a changed woman," Jared joked.

"I'm not falling for the hype," I laughed as I drove back to the police station.

"Protect yourself at all times," Jared joked as he put in his earphones for the drive.

***

I drove into the parking lot and was shocked to see that Madison's car was parked.

"The hell is she doing here?" I chuckled to Jared.

"Shit, I don't know," he answered with a laugh. "That's *your* girl."

"You're right," I laughed as I dialed her number.

No answer.

"She didn't answer," I replied. "I'll try her again once I'm done questioning Jamie," I said.

Jared and I walked into the building and we went in two separate directions.

I walked to the front desk and spoke to Isabella.

I did my routine 'candy snatch' before speaking.

"Isabella, can I get Jamie Perez to interrogation room A34?" I asked her with a chuckle.

"You are going to get enough of taking my candy out of here," Isabella laughed. "Let me get her in the room for you," she called for her over the radio.

"Shoutout to you, Isabella," I started. "You the real MVP," I chuckled as I walked towards the interrogation room.

I walked inside and she was already seated.

"So, Jamie," I stated, "I went over your aunt's house, and all is quiet over there," I told her.

"Was she mad or upset?" Jamie asked me.

I chuckled.

"I'm going to be real with you. I'm the last person that she would express any emotion towards. She knows that I would read her like a book," I took a seat in front of Jamie.

"It's an act," she rebutted. "She's just waiting to hear back from me so there can be repercussions, I know it," Jamie shook her head.

"I'm not going to let that happen," I replied.

A call came over the intercom.

"Detective Young, please report to the front desk," Isabella called out.

"Just my luck, right?" I chuckled to Jamie.

She smiled and I continued.

"I'll be right back," I rose from my chair and left the room.

I started my walk towards the front when I heard a noise from the utility closet. It sounded like something fell.

I looked around and didn't see any nearby officers, so I took my first level of defense and kept my hand on my gun.

I jerked open the door and was left dumbfounded as to what I saw.

I immediately pulled Jared from the room and flung him to the floor like a rag-doll. I got down and began to punch him repeatedly.

"Man, what the fuck are you doing?" I shouted to him. "That's my girl in there and you're supposed to be my fuckin' brother!" I exclaimed.

Jared fought back, which made the objective much harder. But the adrenaline was flowing, and I didn't care how muscular he was or how we evenly matched up, nor did I care who he was; I was hurt at this discovery.

Police officers ran over to break up the fight.
The alarm sounded in the police station and the officers monitoring the interrogation room with Jamie stepped out to see the cause of it.

Since the officers stepped out and she heard the siren, Jamie decided to try to get a quick peek at what was going on.

"You need to stop acting like a little bitch and man up!" Jared shouted and punched me in my nose.

I punched him in his stomach and pulled out my gun and aimed it at his head.

When I drew my weapon, the surrounding officers also pulled out their weapons and aimed them at me.

Since Abel was out sick, Madeline was the next runner up to fill his shoes. She could see that I was hurt and angry, and walked into the crowd.

I looked at Madison. "How are you gonna do this to me? I gave you *everything* your heart desired and this is how you repay me?" I glared at Madison's half-naked body in disgust.

"Richard, don't do this," Madeline replied softly. "Lower your weapon," she ordered.

"I can't do that, Madeline."

"Richard, lower the weapon," she repeated. "Please, don't let this turn ugly and we all do something we will regret."

"You don't understand," I replied. "Me and this man," I glared at Jared while holding my gun to his head, "have been through it all, tracing back to first grade. And then your goofy ass had to do it in the utility closet?" I shouted. "Just earlier we were laughing and joking about some shit we been through, knowing you were creeping with the one I wanted to wife."

I used my free hand and wiped the sweat and tears from my face.

"Man, I'm not fuckin' with y'all no more," I shouted.

I lowered my weapon and unloaded it. I returned it to my holster and walked away.

I started to walk to the front desk.

"Richard, wait," Madison started.

"No. Fuck you and him," I shouted.

While I was walking to the lobby, I could hear all of the murmurs occurring, but I didn't care.

How could they do this to me? In my place of business? In a utility closet? Really?

"Isabella, they told me you needed me here at the lobby," I stated to her.

Isabella didn't know how to respond to me. It was an awkward situation and she couldn't identify the thoughts that were rushing through my mind.

She handed me the first-aid kit for my bruises and abrasions.

"It's fine," she spoke in a low tone.

She, as well as the other officers, had never seen me snap the way I did. It was almost a little embarrassing, but I was too mad to care.

"Do *you* need anything?" Isabella asked me.

"Not unless you can rip my eyes out of the sockets," I joked. I looked at the clock. "I gotta get back to questioning Jamie," I spoke.

"Here, take this," Isabella passed me a pocket-sized container of peroxide and a few gauze pads.

"Thanks, Isabella," I replied.

As I walked back to the interrogation room, I felt as though all eyes were on me; everyone was truly in shock.

I reentered the room and sat back down.

"I'm sorry about that," I spoke to Jamie.

She saw the peroxide and gauze pads in my hand, as well as the bruises and minor cuts on my face. She took the gauze pads and put some peroxide on them.

She dabbed my wounds with the pads.

I was a little concerned that she was touching my face, but I didn't give too much thought to it. I let her care for my wounds.

"I think I've found a way to make this right," I spoke.

Jamie leaned in and kissed me on the lips. I could sense the fireworks going off. It felt so right, although I knew it was wrong; it took my mind off of Madison and Jared for the moment.

Jamie blushed as she retreated from the kiss.

"You're not going to add a sexual harassment charge to the list, are you?" Jamie nervously chuckled.

"Now why in the hell would I do that?" I asked her with a slight laugh.

"I'm sorry, but I like you, Detective," she stated as she played with her hair. "And when I want something, I tend to go for it."

Jamie was beautiful to me, but I already knew how the situation would look and play out if I were to make a move at her.

"I respect that," I replied to her. "You're a go-getter; go on and get what's yours, baby girl," I changed my demeanor. "But I have a plan," I replied.

"Oh, yeah? And what's your plan?" Jamie asked me.

"You want to be cleared, right?" I asked.

"More than anything," she answered.

"Undercover work," I immediately replied. "If you're willing to work with me undercover to catch the real mastermind, I will have them bring your things to the front and walk you out of here, and give you more information," I told her.

Jamie thought for a moment and spoke.

"It could be risky, but if you'll be there to protect me, let's do it," she answered.

Jamie followed me out of the room, to the front desk, and Isabella sent a call for the officers to bring Jamie's things to the front.

Once an officer brought Jamie's belongings to the front, Jared walked side-by-side with Madison before speaking.

"The next time you put a gun to my head, you will regret it," Jared told me, pointing his finger in my face.

I chuckled at Jared and spoke to Isabella.

"Isabella, you have a great rest of the day," I spoke. "Thanks again for the peroxide and pads,"

"Richard, you just take care of yourself, okay?" she told me.

"Will do," I stated as Jamie and I exited the station.

5

I drove towards Jamie's house in silence. She sat in the passenger's seat and twiddled her fingers. I slowed the car down and pulled over to the side of the road and spoke.

"Jamie," I started, "the force can use you as an undercover. You say that Julie is the mastermind. Here's your chance to prove it and to clear your name," I reinforced. "I'll mic you up, and I'll be nearby in case something goes left."

She gave thought to this. I was asking her to go against her aunt: someone that she not only feared but someone who'd helped her when she needed it most.

But she knew that if she didn't do it, she would be in a world of trouble; she knew that no other officer would be willing to cut her a deal.

"When do you want to start, Detective?" she gave in.

"As soon as possible," I answered. "We do need prep time though, and I need to get a better feel for your character," I explained. "How about we get together tonight, 8:00?"

I just wanted an excuse to be able to take her out, to be honest.

She started to blush.

"Detective, are you asking me out?"

"I'm just trying to get a better feel of who you are," I semi-lied and smiled.

Jamie looked at the time and noticed it was noon.

"Detective, I'm flattered —"

"Richard," I spoke in my everyday tone. "Call me Richard."

"Richard, I'm flattered..." She stated.

"Then join me, tonight. 8:00, so I can further explain."

Jamie wanted to go out with me as badly as I wanted to go out with her, so she decided to go along with my moves.

"Okay," she sighed. "Now remember, Richard, this is business," she told me with a chuckle and small wink.

"A man of my word," I chuckled.

I knew at this point that it would be too late to turn back and reverse my decision, but I had confidence in the choices that I was making.

I started to drive again, and I drove until I arrived at Jamie's house.

"Thank you for the ride, Richard. I'll see you tonight," she smiled and disappeared into the house.

I knew that I was taking a risk in letting her out of my sight; for all I knew, she could leave town, but I had faith in my decision and her, although I hardly knew her. Maybe my thoughts were cloudy because of what just occurred with Jared and Madison.

***

I got in my car and was on my way home to get dressed when Abel called me.

"Hello," I answered.

"You need to let me know what happened," he immediately said.

I knew right away that word had gotten back to him about Jared and me.

"Roberts, it's a sensitive subject. I'm leaving to see why I'm called to the front, and these two are naked in a utility closet. That's supposed to be my boy," I spoke.

"I know you and Jared are going through some things because of this, but that doesn't mean you are excused from working with him. You have a job to do. Don't let this affect your job. You have been promoted and now other officers will be looking to you for everything. Everything you do affects everything and everyone in the squad," he told me. "You have to be the example, Richard."

Once he started using first names with me, I knew it was serious.

"I understand, Roberts," I replied.

"Now, since we've gotten that cleared up, where are you now?" Abel asked me.

"I'm on my way home. I'm taking the rest of the day off; I seriously need it to clear my mind," I admitted to Abel. "Plus, I'm meeting up with Jamie tonight at the *House of Soul* to review everything."

"The *House of Soul*? That's a very fancy place," Abel chuckled. "No way this is 'just business'. Sounds to me like you're flirting with death," he laughed.

"It's not even like that, Roberts," I laughed. "I'll be safe. I promise."

"What about good?" he chuckled.

I knew what he was referencing, so I just laughed.

"Talk to you soon," he chuckled. "Let me know how it goes."

"Will do," I responded.

I drove until I reached home, and quickly went inside.

I only had a few hours to mentally prepare myself for what was to come.

Once I finished my shower, I decided what to wear.

The first suit that I picked out, I decided it was too formal, and the second suit I chose wasn't right for the occasion. I picked out one more suit: black, with diamond cuff links. It had a white shirt and a black tie. This was perfect, not too formal, and not too dressy. I put on the suit and grabbed my gun, badge, and phone off of my dresser.

I exited my home and made sure all of my doors were locked.

I entered my vehicle and drove towards Jamie's home. I couldn't get my mind off the kiss with Jamie earlier.

I knew I shouldn't have been feeling any kind of way towards her, especially considering the current conditions, but it was something about her that I trusted.

Once I arrived at Jamie's house, I got out of my car and waited beside it; perfect timing for my phone to ring.

"Hello," I answered.

"Young, I was informed that they are wrapping up with the case that occurred at the John Hancock building. They got some of the suspects in custody, and just want for you to confirm the identities," Abel spoke.

"Roberts, I can't do it tonight," I chuckled. "You know I'm meeting with Jamie. But I'll get to it the first chance I get," I told him.

"Oh, that's right, you have your date tonight," he laughed. "Let me let you get to it," he joked. "Just keep your phone on in case you need to be reached."

"I got you, Roberts," I chuckled. "But I'm gonna get back at you in a bit," I mentioned as I saw Jamie emerge from the house

"Okay, cool. Talk to you soon," Abel replied.

Jamie was in a cream-colored dress, not too baggy and not too tight. The dress firmly hugged her body and accentuated her curves.

She had on mascara, just the right amount, and she had on red lipstick. I could tell she was one who truly put a lot of energy into her appearance.

I walked up to the patio. "Where are you headed to, looking this beautiful?" I asked her, jokingly.

"If that's your way of complimenting me, thank you," she chuckled with a blush. "You look rather dapper yourself," she smiled.

I held out my hand for her to take. Once she took my hand, we walked down the steps and to my vehicle.

I opened the passenger door and climbed inside. I gently closed her door and walked back over to the driver's side, got inside, and started the engine.

"I hope you enjoy yourself tonight," I told her as I started to drive. "Even though, we're all about business tonight," I chuckled.

"I'm sure I will," she chuckled as she put her hand on top of mine.

I drove until I reached the restaurant. I parked the vehicle, and then I walked back over to Jamie's side to show my chivalrous ways. Again, she took my hand and I walked her inside.

I looked at my watch; it was 8:00 exactly. The greeter got us seated right away and told us to wait for our server. I looked over and I saw none other than Madison and Jared sitting at a table right across from us; anger filled my body.

The waiter came by; I let Jamie order her food and I ordered mine after her. The drinks were the first to arrive.

"This place is beautiful," Jamie stated after she sipped her wine. "I'm glad I came."

"I'm glad you came too, Jamie," I told her while I decided to sip my wine. "Jamie, if you're serious about clearing your name, you have to work with me and my unit," I told her as I decided to change the subject onto the business part of the evening.

"What exactly would you need me to do?" she asked.

"Well, as I said, a lot of criminals act differently when police are around; they act as if they've changed. But let's say they thought you were a normal pedestrian; they wouldn't act any different, which is why we need you. And you are access to the prime suspect: Julie Wilson," I replied.

"But what if she finds out I'm helping you?" Jamie asked as her voice started to crack.

"That's why I will be there. Not physically right beside you, but I will be just circling the block. I won't let anything happen, Jamie," I mentioned as I wiped the few tears that accumulated in her eyes.

At this moment, I knew that she was a really sensitive and sweet person, and she couldn't have possibly pulled that stunt on her own.

"Will you help me help you, Jamie?"

She sighed, "what do I have to do?"

"Jamie, well first you will have to give me a jacket Julie sees you wear often or something of that nature. I will have our experts bug it and whenever you go over your aunt's home, I will be able to hear and see whatever it is you hear and see," I answered.

"I can give you the jacket I brought with us, but it's in the car," she spoke.

"That works," I replied. "I'll drop it off early tomorrow morning and it should be fully bugged by tomorrow evening."

She took my hands in hers.

"I'm not going to do this with just any officer," she started. "Promise me you'll be there," she demanded.

I couldn't help but admire the sparkle in her eye as she spoke.

"I promise," I responded.

The waiter brought us the food, and we ate and spoke about everything from what led up to the Hancock incident, to our love lives, and personal beliefs.

Forty-five minutes later, the DJ of the restaurant had announced that the dance floor was now open and that he would be taking requests for the evening.

"You gotta love this scene," Jamie smiled.

"Yeah, it is pretty amazing," I replied. "I'll be right back," I told her.

I walked up to the DJ and spoke to him.

I handed him a $20 bill. And the song faded from Alicia Keys' *No One*, to *Slow Jam* by Usher.

I walked back over to Jamie.

"Would you like to dance, Jamie?" I asked her.

"I'd love to," she responded as she took my hand.

I walked her over to the middle of the dance floor and she put one arm around my right shoulder and took my right hand in her left; leaving my left arm to go around her waist.

She rested her head on my chest. I listened to the lyrics as we danced.

> *I was all alone*
> *I was feeling rather low*
> *I needed someone to*
> *lift my spirits up*
> *So, I dropped in on a dance*
> *Just to take a glance*
> *and there this lovely thing was*
> *She was more than enough*
> *I asked her for her hand*
> *Said would you like to dance*
> *So pleased that I had asked*
> *She quickly took my hand*
> *And we danced and fell in love*
> *On a slow jam*

Jamie hugged me tighter as she continued to dance but kept her head rested on my chest.

Something about this situation felt so right; I was making her feel safe and comfortable, but I also felt comfortable with her. Perhaps I felt like I knew her because of her connection to Julie, or maybe it was something in the universe.

"Are you okay, Jamie?" I asked her with a smile.

"Yes," she whispered and adjusted her head.

"I'm glad," I told her and I kissed her on the forehead.

I further listened to the lyrics, keeping the rhythm of the dance.

I've been trying to find someone who
I could give my good lovin' to
Never did I dream I'd find someone
I've been tryin' to find someone, too
I prayed to heaven and then I found you
I swear I fell in love the night you
Danced into my heart
Play another slow jam, this time make it sweet
On a slow jam, for me and my baby

There were hundreds of people around, but it felt as though Jamie and I were the only ones in the room. The song ended and I hugged Jamie tighter. When I looked at her, she had a few tears on her face.

"Jamie, baby, why the tears?" I asked her.

Whoops. I let 'baby' slip out. Oh well, I couldn't take it back.

"I'm just happy, yet I'm also worried. I'm having a wonderful time here with you, Richard, but I'm not going to lie: I'm worried about this whole thing with my aunt," she admitted.

"I'm glad, Jamie. Please don't worry, it's not good to stress. Everything will be fine and I'll keep you safe," I responded.

She looked at me blankly.

"I promise," I added.

Seconds passed before she spoke again.

"Thank you," she whispered to me.

I took Jamie's hand and we walked back to the table. We both took our seats and sat there admiring the elegance of the restaurant. It was something about Jamie; I couldn't exactly pinpoint what it was, but something attracted me to her.

Jared approached my table and spoke.

"So, this is what we're doing now?" he chuckled. "We're bringing criminals out to dinner?"

I could tell that Jamie was offended.

"Jared, take ya' ass somewhere else," I stated to him trying not to ruin my night.

"Nah, but on some real shit, can I talk to you for a minute, Rick?"

"What could we have to talk about?" I laughed.

"For real," Jared spoke with a serious tone.

"Bruh, go on back over to your date. I'm not in the mood for this shit right now."

"So, you're going to blow off the situation like it didn't happen. And for what?" he looked at Jamie. "For a bitch who wanted to kill your ass?"

I immediately rose to my feet and shoved him.

"What the hell is wrong with you?" I asked him.

I followed the question with a violent shove.

He stumbled a little bit and pushed me back. Regaining my balance, I punched him in the face.

Members of the restaurant got up to try to break it up.

"The fuck are you coming over here being disrespectful for?" I asked as I punched him again.

Restaurant security ran over and intervened.

They stopped me from hitting Jared by grabbing my arms.

They pulled me from him.

"Alright you two, you are both out of here. Pay your bill and leave." The security guard told us.

I roughly ripped my arm from the security guard's grip.

"Come on, Jamie," I told her and I left two hundred-dollar bills on the table, even though I knew the bill would be much less.

I took her hand and together we left out of the restaurant.

"Are you okay, Jamie?" I asked. "I'm so sorry."

"I'm fine," she replied. "You have no reason to apologize," she gently spoke.

I opened the door and Jamie climbed inside of the car. I walked over to my side, got inside, and started the vehicle.

"I truly loved tonight. I had the best time of my life," she replied with a smile.

Jamie leaned in and kissed me passionately. We sat inside of the car, lips locked for about thirty seconds. We finally retreated from the kiss, slowly; neither of us wanted it to end.

"Honestly, I enjoyed myself." She smiled at me.

The moment I pulled out of the parking lot, the rain started to fall from the sky.

Jamie and I continued to talk.

"So, what made this evening so special?" I asked her.

"Well, if you want a truthful answer," she started, "I really enjoyed just being with you. Something about you makes me feel so safe and good," she smiled. "I even enjoyed the dance, even though you have two left feet," she laughed.

"Maybe, it's the fact I'm a detective and carry the gun around," I told her laughing. "And nah, baby, I don't have two left feet. You just couldn't keep up with my smooth moves," I joked.

Jamie laughed.

"No, it's not even that. Even if you weren't a detective or had a gun, I think I would feel safe around you," she told me.

I continued the drive as I kept my high beams on. The rain came down harder.

"Richard," Jamie stated, "when I first kissed you, what did you think?" she asked. I could tell she was blushing from the question.

"Honestly, I felt relieved. Like, I was relieved from the stress that had just come to me. I was happy because of the kiss, but shocked at the same time because I wasn't expecting it."

"How was it?" she asked. I could tell she was getting more and more embarrassed with each question.

"The kiss," I thought for a second, "it was amazing Jamie. It was like I was in a firework experience; that exciting feeling that you get as they explode," I told her.

"So, if you had to compare it to the kiss you had just gotten, which one would you choose?" she further asked me.

I was careful with my answer; well, I tried to be. Something about tonight and being with Jamie broke my thick skin.

"It would be hard to choose because I want them all." I flirted.

She was blushing harder than ever now.

I kept driving on the expressway and I drove past the exit to her house.

"Baby, we passed my exit," she told me.

"I know, Jamie. Just sit back and relax and enjoy the ride," I gently smiled at her.

She looked at me inquisitively, smiled, and kissed me on my cheek.

I drove for miles and I eventually came to a gentle stop. I turned off the ignition and took off my jacket. I held it in my hand and walked over to Jamie's door and opened it.

"Hand please, miss?" I stated with a French accent.

Jamie chuckled. "Why, certainly!" She gave me her hand and I helped her out of the car. I put the jacket over her shoulders because it was chilly outside.

We walked over to the edge of the cliff, near the water, and looked up.

"Don't you just love the stars in a clear night sky?" Jamie asked me.

"Yes, I love beautiful nights like this," I responded with a smile.

"What do you think the stars represent?" Jamie asked me.

I thought about the corniest way to reply.

"The stars are a reflection," I responded.

"Of what?" She asked, curious as to what I had to say.

I turned and faced her.

"Of the sparkle in your eye," I told her.

Jamie started to blush again and kissed me on the cheek. "Such a romantic," she giggled. "It takes more than that to win me over," she added.

"Oh really?" I joked. "Well, who's to say that I'm trying to win you over?" I chuckled.

She rolled her eyes.

"It's just a feeling that I'm getting. And, the fact that you haven't been able to take your eyes off me says wonders," Jamie smiled.

"Well, maybe you just have something on your face," I chuckled. "Remember, this is just business."

"What kind of business?" she asked. "Do you mean *this* kind of business?" she placed her lips upon mine as I put my hands around her waist.

"Oh yeah, all business," I stated as I looked at her, admiringly.

She smiled and held my hand.

I hugged her tightly and we stood there, looking at the stars.

Minutes later, I got a blanket out of the trunk and laid it on the sand. I walked back over to Jamie, took her hand again, and walked her over to the blanket.

We both sat down and continued to talk.

"What would you consider this to be, Jamie?" I asked her. "A first date?"

"Eh, something like that," she added, smiling.

"Well, is this what you would call a 'perfect first date'?"

"No better way to end a date than a night on the beach," she told me. "Memories like this last a lifetime."

"They could... if they're spent with the right person." I told her, and I took her hands into mine.

"Aw, *que lindo*," she spoke.

"Oh, you speak Spanish?" I asked her.

I heard her accent, but I didn't want to just assume that she spoke Spanish without confirmation.

"Puerto Rican blood runs through my veins," she spoke.

"There's so much we need to know about each other," I added.

We sat and chatted for another thirty minutes before I decided it was time to go.

I looked over and Jamie had rested her head on me and fell asleep. I picked her up in my arms like a baby and gently placed her in the car. I put on her seat belt and walked over to my side. I put on my seat belt and drove off.

***

Moments later I arrived at Jamie's house.

She was still asleep, but I didn't want to wake her up. I reached in her coat pocket and grabbed her keys and opened my side of the car. I walked around to her side and opened the door and picked her up. Although she was asleep, her hands wrapped around my neck as I held her.

I walked her to the door and I unlocked it. I walked in the house, with her in my arms still. I was surprised that she didn't have a security light of some sort to help guide her in the house.

I walked her upstairs to her room and inside the room was beautiful. It looked like nothing I'd ever seen before. Her bed was so neatly and perfectly made, her TV: a 64-inch flat-screen, and for her light, there was an overhead chandelier.

I walked her to the bed and placed her down. I kissed her on her forehead and she started to wake up. She opened her eyes fully and saw me standing there.

"Hey, baby," she started. "Where are we?" she asked.

"I brought you home, Jamie," I told her.

"I knew this bed felt familiar," she chuckled.

I laughed.

"I'm about to go," I told her.

"Richard, thank you. I had the most wonderful time tonight," she told me.

"You're welcome, Jamie," I told her with a smile.

I kissed her on the cheek and left out the house.

I closed her door and locked it from the inside before getting in my car.

I reflected on the evening and I found myself smiling. Although this was supposed to be a business date, it turned out to be more intimate than expected.

Everything went perfectly, aside from what occurred with Jared. Now, I had to get my head on straight for the next day of work.

6

I walked into my office the next day and was greeted by a stack of folders.

Abel walked into my office. His arm was in a sling and cast.

"Had fun last night?" he asked me.

I laughed at him.

"It was all business," I chuckled.

"That much, I know is a lie," Abel laughed. "But that's only part of the reason I came by. I really want to speak to you about Jared."

Abel sat on my desk.

"And, I'm assuming a chair is too much to ask for," I joked.

"Should I sit in one?" he asked.

"It's your life," I rebutted with a smirk.

Abel laughed at my joke.

"No, but seriously, I want you to tell me what happened with Jared," he began.

I looked down and twiddled my fingers before looking up again.

"I'm hearing gossip from other officers and I got word from Isabella about what occurred, and I've spoken to Jared, but I want to know things from your side of the story," Abel added.

I sighed.

"While I was interrogating Jamie," I began, "I was called over the intercom. I heard a noise in the utility closet, so I went and checked it out."

"Keep going," Abel spoke.

"When I opened the door, I saw Jared tonguing down my girlfriend," I shook my head.

Abel put his head down and put his hand over his face.

"So, I blacked out, honestly. It was like I was possessed. I pulled him out and started beating on him."

Abel shook his head in disbelief.

"That bad over a girl?" he questioned.

"And then I ran into him last night. Can you believe he and Madison were out on a date, just hours after the altercation?" I chuckled. "Let's just say that didn't end so well."

Abel adjusted his collar.

"Last I checked, you all have been cool since first grade, so something had to truly go wrong for you to feel this way."

"You're damn right, it did," I replied. "Once I saw what I saw, I snapped," I remembered the sight of Madison and Jared in the closet being intimate.

I switched subjects.

"What's up with these folders?" I asked Abel as I flipped through one of them.

"When you have some shit go down," Abel stated, "you get hit with paperwork," he chuckled.

I thought he was referring to what happened with Jared.

"You know what happened at the Hancock building? Merry Christmas," he said.

I looked at the papers and back up at him.

"So, this is what it's like to be top cop?" I asked.

He laughed and headed for the door.

"Young," he turned slightly, "keep a level head about this whole Hubbard situation. You know the force needs you."

"I'll keep my head," I replied.

Abel tapped on my door and left the room. He closed the door to my office before disappearing.

I started to look through one of the folders and I saw paperwork on the entire incident.

"I don't feel like doing this shit today," I laughed aloud.

I sorted the documents in the folder and turned on some music.

***

An hour or so later, I was wrapping up the paperwork, so I decided to give Jamie a call. I hadn't spoken to her all day and I wanted to ensure everything was alright with her.

"Hello?" she answered.

"Hey, Jamie, it's Richard," I told her while I put away the folders.

"Hey, you," she spoke excitedly. "I slept so well last night," she continued.

"That's terrific," I told her. "Did you have anything specific that you dreamt about?" I asked her.

"Oh, nothing much," she stated. "Just this girl who grew up in hard conditions and then grew up to find and meet this wonderful man, who treated her like a queen," Jamie told me.

"Sounds familiar; I think I may have had the same dream," I told her with a chuckle. "Except, I think the dream I had was about the man rescuing her from bad conditions."

"It was an amazing dream," she replied.

"It sounds like it was terrific," I told her. "What are you up to today?" I asked as I locked the drawer.

"I know I have to go to the dry cleaners and then I don't really know," she spoke.

I looked at my computer and an email came through, I read it as I continued to speak to Jamie.

"How about you?" she asked.

"Well I'm here at the office now; I just finished filing these papers and now I'm about to go downstairs and meet with a few officers. After that, I'm on the road patrolling, as far as I know," I told her. "And, I just got an email confirming that they've finished with your jacket, so I'll be picking that up today as well."

Officer Burke walked into the room.

"Hold on, Jamie," I told her and placed the call on hold. "Yes, Burke?" I addressed him.

"Young, they need you downstairs regarding what occurred with Hubbard yesterday, and what occurred at the Hancock building."

"Okay, well I'm almost finished here. I'll be down as soon as I'm finished," I replied.

Officer Burke left out of the room.

"Sorry about that, Jamie."

"It's okay," she replied.

A second reminder came through my computer about the jacket and Jamie continued to speak.

"Richard, there's something very different about you. Very different than with other guys I've dated," she said.

"Oh yeah? Like what?" I asked her.

"Okay, well for starters, every other guy I've dated would always bring me home and expect to stay the night. And then, when I didn't allow them to stay, they leave irritated and don't ever call back. But with you, you didn't expect it to happen. You made sure I was safe, protected, well, and happy throughout the whole date. You never made any sexual references or advances towards me," Jamie mentioned. "Which is a little concerning," she admitted. "Because let's face it, all men come for something," she added.

"Sometimes that is all you need. You may just need for someone to have your best interest at hand," I told her. "Some men come to restore. I don't want you for sex."

"I guess that time will tell, huh? We have to take it one step at a time."

"I'm game for that, Jamie," I stated.

Isabella called for me over the intercom and I spoke to Jamie again.

"Jamie, they are calling for me to go downstairs," I told her. "So, I'm going to call you back, okay?" I told her.

"You promise?" she asked me with a chuckle.

"Cross my heart. I promise," I told Jamie.

"Okay, Richard. Call me later," she responded.

"I will," I replied.

I hung up the phone and picked up my badge. I locked my office and walked to the huddle room.

Several officers stood around the room. Jared was on the opposing end.

Abel entered the room behind me and instructed Jared and me to both have a seat.

I sat on one end of the table and Jared sat on the opposite side.

Abel cleared his throat.

"Okay, so you two need to come to some kind of understanding. You are two of our top officers, and we can't have your heads all rattled because of personal issues," he spoke.

"Abel, it's not even just a personal issue. He brought the problem into the workplace," I replied.

Jared glared at me.

"That's another thing I wanted to discuss. Certain things shouldn't ever be brought into the workplace," he spoke. "What happened, from my understanding, is to *never* happen again, from any of you," he spoke to all of the officers.

None of the officers spoke; they presented a look of confirmation.

"Now, I want for you all to shake hands and drop this feud," Abel spoke.

Moments of silence passed and neither Jared nor I dared to move.

"Can't shake his hand, Roberts," I spoke. "A handshake isn't going to make this shit right," I finished.

"You're damn right, it won't," Jared asserted.

"If you want to get big and bad, we can take this shit outside," I aggressed.

"This is not about to happen," Abel raised his tone. "Now, I can't tell you that everything is going to be alright. That's not why I'm here. But damn it, we have a job to do and that's to keep this city safe, and we can't do that if you all are letting a personal situation interfere with work."

I controlled my breathing and calmed down.

"It's evident that this personal feud isn't going to end today or anytime soon. I can't just let the two of you go, to be honest," Abel spoke. "You two are amongst the top performing officers. But," he started. "You all have taken an oath to protect this city, and you all have to make an oath to me that you will deal with this outside of work and not let it linger here inside of the workplace. If it does, I will suspend both of you. I promise you that." Abel looked at Jared and me.

I thought for a moment. I loved my job and I didn't want to even risk losing it over something like this.

Jared and I simultaneously reached our hands over the table and connected.

"Alright, then," Abel replied as we both pulled our hands apart. "Richard, what's the status with Jamie?" he asked.

"She's willing to work with us to keep her record clean. She tells me that Julie is responsible, and I believe her," I spoke.

"As long as you don't let your personal interest affect your professional expertise," Jared replied.

"Don't be a smartass," I rebutted.

"Chill out," Abel interrupted.

He looked at Jared and then back at me.

"So, what's the next move?" he asked.

"I'm getting her jacket bugged," I replied. "I'll be picking that up in a little bit."

"Well," Abel started to rise to his feet, "if you're finished with that paperwork, I'll let you get to it."

I rose from my seat and walked to the door. Although Jared and I had just shaken hands, I knew right away that this wouldn't be the end of our issues.

I stepped out of the room and pulled out my phone. I walked to my car while goofily smiling at my phone.

I got into my car and left the parking lot. I drove until I reached the location that they were rigging Jamie's jacket.

I entered the room and pulled my badge from my coat pocket. The secretary directed me to a room and I entered.

"Detective Young," Melissa called out as she emerged from the back.

"Hey, Melissa, how'd the jacket go?" I asked her.

"Well, we were able to bug it for you. I tried to ensure it was as discreet as possible, and I took the liberty of putting a GPS chip into it."

She showed me the receiver on the teeth of the zipper track.

"Multiple receivers, so that if a tooth goes missing from the track, there will still be a way to pull a connection."

She directed my attention to the laptop on the table beside her. I saw a map and a marker speared over our current location.

"And, if you click on it," Melissa clicked the icon, "it will give you an approximate address."

"You all really outdid yourself with this," I chuckled. "Now, how about hearing the microphone and seeing the camera?"

Melissa laughed.

"It's simple. Just rub your finger or hand over the right collar." She ran her finger over the collar and a notification appeared on the screen, alerting that one of the recording devices had been activated. "Click on the alert, and you will see and or hear everything that the jacket sees."

"That's it, Melissa? We don't have to keep this thing charged so that the GPS works?" I chuckled.

"Yes, that's it," she laughed. "It runs on a battery, but the one we're putting in the equipment is going to last for at least a year before it needs to be recharged or replaced," she explained. "Just install this disc to your laptop and you'll be good to go. The program allows you to record to your system as well if you need evidence. Oh, and take this earpiece as well. Just a little something for your UC to wear to communicate with you."

"Thanks, Melissa," I told her while I got the jacket, the small earpiece, and the disc.

I left the building, got in my car, and called Jamie before driving off. The first time, she didn't answer. I called her back, but this time she answered in a whisper.

"Hello," she whispered.

"Jamie? What's wrong?" I asked her.

I listened closely to see if I could identify anything out of the ordinary and point out the reason for her whispering.

"Julie. She's here. I can't talk right now," she told me and hung up.

I didn't have an opportunity to say anything further before she hung up.

I started the car and sped in the direction of Jamie's house.

I couldn't help but think the worse as I sped to Jamie's house. I worried about the possibilities if I didn't arrive at her home in time.

I pulled up to her house and I quickly exited the vehicle with my gun drawn. I pressed my ear against the door and I could hear Jamie crying. I aimed my gun and I kicked the door, opening it.

I didn't make any noise as I walked through the home and following the sounds of her cries.

I entered a room and saw her on the floor crying. Glass was broken all around her, but I didn't see any signs of blood.

I kneeled and put my gun in the holster.

"Jamie, are you okay?" I asked, softly.

She quickly hugged me. "I'm glad you're here," she stated.

She attempted to stop crying, but she couldn't.

"What happened?" I asked her as I tried to console her.

"My aunt came by and had a 'talk' with me," the tears continued to roll down Jamie's cheeks.

I wiped her face with my shirt. "Why'd you put the quotes around talk?" I asked her. "Tell me what happened."

Jamie began to explain what happened while flashing back to the conversation she had with her aunt, moments before.

"*Jamie, it doesn't make sense. I've spent my life training you how to successfully complete a drop. Why and how'd you get caught and arrested?'* Julie asked me.

'I'm sorry, Auntie. But there was no way I would escape. At least 20 police cars were behind me and then the helicopters started to come in; two officers from the helicopter shot at my car, they pretty much killed my engine with their bullets.'

'What did I tell you? With a case like this, police will be all over you. This includes helicopters, tanks, squad cars, everything. And when they shoot at your car, slow down, but do not press the brakes, and if the bullets connect, keep your head down and keep driving forward. But, at least you're out now. Which officer arrested you?' Julie asked me."

"What happened after that, Jamie?" I asked her. She continued to tell me what happened."

"*'Detective Young,'* I told her.

'Richard? And he just let you go? Last time I checked he was a tougher cookie to break,' my aunt replied. *'Look at me, Jamie: don't ever trust Richard! And if he tries to arrest you on the next drop, don't just stand there, resist like you've never resisted before,'* she laughed.

'But they had guns aimed everywhere; if I resisted I would be shot and killed.' I told her and I dared not mention what we had going on.

'Jamie, officers will not shoot you unless you pose a threat to them,' she told me.

'But, Richard was nice. He actually stopped the SWAT team members from roughly pulling on me and possibly killing me.'

I guess she wasn't too fond of me defending the cop who put her away. This is when I could tell she got infuriated," Jamie said. "She didn't hit me, but she decided to break things around the room.

'Don't ever say that again,' she started. *'Richard is the lowest of the low. Do not get involved with him.'* She then inhaled sharply. *'Jamie, now you know your Aunt Julie loves you, and everything I do and say is for a reason,'* Julie stated, before leaving

here. And the whole time, all I could wonder is 'where's Ricky?'," Jamie spoke.

I felt a little bad that I wasn't there to protect her from her aunt.

"I'm here, Jamie. Don't worry," I reassured her. "I got the jacket finished and I'll technically be with you at all times that you have on the jacket or it's near you," I spoke and kissed her on the forehead.

Jamie burst into tears and gave me another hug. "Thank you," she told me.

I hugged Jamie back and walked outside to get her jacket. I gave her the jacket and explained how it worked. I also gave her the earpiece.

"It's simple, I told her. All you have to do is rub your finger over the right collar to activate the GPS, camera, and microphone," I explained to her before I heard my name being called over the police radio.

"I have to go, Jamie. I'll give you a call later," I told her with a smile.

"Thank you, Ricky. Thank you for coming by and keeping me safe."

"It's my job, Jamie, remember?" I told her with a slight chuckle.

"Oh wow," she replied with a laugh. "Well, even if it wasn't your job as an officer, would you have still come by for me?"

"Normally, I don't make house calls," I joked, "but for you, I'd make an exception. You know what I'm thinking though?" I asked.

"What's that?" she asked.

"Protective custody. This situation with Julie is quickly getting out of control," I spoke.

"We can discuss it," Jamie replied. "Go on back to work, Officer," she smirked as she kissed me on the cheek.

"Detective Young, to you," I chuckled.

She laughed.

"No comment. Be safe, baby," she walked closer.

"Don't come any closer, Jamie, or else I'm gonna have to arrest you for not being able to finish what you start," I told her. "For that, and for being so beautiful," I told her.

She came closer and I kissed her.

"Bye, Jamie," I told her and walked out of her house.

7

Jamie and I had been dating and working together for a few months and things were beginning to get serious. No longer did I only see her as a witness to catching Julie, but I started catching feelings for her.

I did my best to keep a professional relationship with Jamie around other officers, which I feel worked for the most part, but quite a few officers could tell something was going on between us.

I got in my car and I received a transmission on my radio.
"Lead units in the 26th district; please make your way to the station."
I drove to the station while thinking of what was the purpose of the transmission.
Once I arrived at the station, I was approached by Abel.

"Young, we have to go to this meeting. I'm going to let you in before everyone else. We have a feeling that what happened before, at the Hancock Building, is going to happen again. But we don't have exact proof. But we feel this one will be bigger and more dangerous," Abel told me as we walked.

"Way ahead of you, I got Jamie's jacket bugged and just awaiting proof. She's still working with us, Cap," I told him.

"So, you're really thinking that Julie is responsible, huh?"

"I know she is, Roberts."

We proceeded into the room for the meeting.

***

Once I exited the building, I got in my vehicle and turned on my laptop.

I launched the application that was used for surveillance and saw that there was no connection. I assumed Jamie hadn't turned on the surveillance features on her jacket.

I dialed her number.

She answered on the first ring.

"Hello," she spoke into the phone; her voice sounded beautiful.

"Hey, baby," I spoke. "I just left the station."

She knew that there was work to be done.

"Okay, babe. What's going on?" she asked.

"Jamie, I need you to go to your aunt's house. We need more info on if there will be a new drop. I'll be right around the corner."

I could hear Jamie sigh.

"Okay, Ricky. As long as you promise to be right there."

"I'll be right there in case something goes sour, babe. Don't forget to turn on the surveillance on your jacket."

"Okay, babe," she spoke before hanging up.

I began the drive to Julie's home while keeping my laptop open for the connection from Jamie.

Jamie activated the surveillance on the jacket and I could see what she saw.

"I hope you can hear me," she spoke aloud and sighed.

"I can hear you loud and clear, baby," I spoke as I continued the drive.

Jamie got in her car and drove to her aunt's house. Upon arrival, Julie opened the door.

"Jamie, what a surprise."

Jamie embraced her aunt after she walked inside.

"Aunt Julie, I want to know more about this drop. How will it go?" Jamie asked her.

Julie approached Jamie and I slowed the car down to pull over.

"Ah, so you're anxious to know now?" she asked Jamie. "I hope you've been preparing physically."

Jamie chuckled.

"Yes, I have, Auntie."

"Let's get outta this jacket first," she told Jamie, suspicious of the unexpected arrival.

"She never was stupid," I spoke to myself as I saw her approach Jamie.

I reached into the center console and retrieved my badge.

"No, I'm a little cold," Jamie responded.

"Well, Jamie I'll turn up the heat, let's take off this jacket."

I put my hand on my holster to get a grip on my weapon.

Jamie knew how her aunt wouldn't be willing to back down, so she removed her jacket and hung it on the banister. She positioned the jacket so that the camera was facing her and Julie.

She left the earpiece, which resembled a Bluetooth, in her ear.

I locked my car door and secured the gun to my waist. I put the car in drive and drove down the block. I continued to listen to Julie's plan as she explained it to Jamie.

"Jamie, for this drop, you have to be very careful. This drop will have tanks, squad cars, police dogs, regular vehicles, and everything; shit could get you killed," Julie started.

I pressed record on the software and the audio started to record.

"Now, the drop is in two days," Julie pulled out a blueprint and began to show Jamie how it was all planned out.

"You will be standing here, on top of the high-rise building. This is an office building and we need to bring it down to the ground. Don't ask me why," Julie chuckled. "It's just an order."

She continued to explain.

"No one will be present in the building; it will be completely empty; not even the cleaning crew. There will be a bottled explosive in the trash can near the south door. Be sure to light the papers in the trash can to ignite the explosive causing a diversion and helping to draw the police to the top floor."

Jamie nodded her head yes while trying her hardest to not look at the camera. I knew she was nervous and wasn't sure if the equipment is working, so I spoke in the earpiece.

"I see you, Jamie. I'm right here."

She continued to nod her head as Julie spoke, but I know she was also nodding to confirm that she could hear me.

"This is when I will make the 9-1-1call and ask for the police. I expect the police to arrive there within minutes and I'm sure Richard will show up, so quickly run downstairs to meet the masked man on the motorcycle at the rear of the building; he will give you a package," she circled a man on the paper. "This package is a more powerful explosive rigged to detonate on a timer. Be careful with this package, as it also has smaller explosives on the side of them. You will need to take these explosives off and place 2 of the 6 on the two corners of the building, close to the elevator; don't worry about the rest, you will send them up in the elevator."

I zoomed in on the camera to try to get a better glimpse of the paper. I saw Jamie's hands shaking and a few beads of sweat accumulating.

"Jamie, control your shaking. Don't be nervous. We don't want to raise any red flags," I spoke over her earpiece.

I didn't expect a response from her, but she slightly nodded her head to show affirmation.

"You should take the south stairwell down to the garage; wait for my signal and then place the explosive in the elevator and send it up to the 24th floor. This will give you time to get out of the building before it blows. Officers may be covering all entry and exits to the building, so this mission requires you to be stealthy. You follow all of this, Jamie?" Julie asked her.

"Yes, Auntie. I understand so far, but I have a question," Jamie stated.

"What's up?"

"If you're going to be there, why am I doing all of the dirty work?" Jamie chuckled although she was nervous about her aunt's response.

"I'm training *you* to become the brains of the family. I'm fresh out of jail. I'm not in any hurry to go back. But let's say I were to do this, what happens if I'm caught by the police or even worse: what if I'm killed? Your income comes to a halt and who knows what's next. You may end up becoming a drunk or a druggie, but that shit's not gonna work out," Julie laughed. "Have you seen your physical condition?" she couldn't stop laughing. "I'm just playing, Jamie, but seriously, I'm trying to teach you. Besides, I won't physically be there; I'll be miles away."

Jamie looked at her aunt inquisitively.

"But, how do you expect for me to effectively pull this off with so many officers surrounding me?"

Julie took a moment to think, before proceeding.

"See these stick figures," Julie started as she drew three stick figures. "Consider these to be 'Tom, Dick, and Harry', but there are multiple copies of them. In other words, there will be more chaos surrounding you, so all eyes will not be on you. Plus, we're hoping that the explosions will create enough diversions to get them out of the way. If we're lucky, you'll be able to become invisible to the police."

"I guess," Jamie spoke reluctantly. "Continue."

Julie continued explaining.

"Now, when you receive the signal that the package has been received, your job is not over. You need to lure Detective Young towards the building, but remember, time will be winding down and with each second, you will be closer to the bomb exploding. Get him to one of the corners of the building, but you need to time it so that as he crosses the bomb, it will explode. All of the bombs will be set to explode within 5 minutes of the rigging. My guesstimate is that by the time you start to lure Detective Young to the building, you'll be down to 10 seconds. Let's face reality; Detective Young will not be the only officer coming after you, so the more officers caught in the blast, the better. You just make sure that you can get out of the situation and if they corner you, you're screwed, baby girl. Get out of the situation and I need you to get in the get-away car and drive away. If you do this successfully, you will have twenty thousand dollars coming your way. Not from me, but some close friends." Julie finished.

I could tell that Jamie had to be shocked by the amount of money being rewarded for this, as I was shocked myself. I just hoped that she wouldn't be tempted by it.

"Auntie, do you think I'm physically able to complete this task?" Jamie asked.

"Jamie, of course. As long as you follow my instructions. You have been doing the workout routines I've given you, right?"

"Yes."

"As long as you've been doing them, I'm sure you're in shape to do this. Look at me," Julie spoke to Jamie.

Jamie looked Julie in her eyes.

"I plan and execute missions for a living. Follow my advice and it's smooth sailing."

Jamie slightly shook her head.

"Got that ass, Julie," I whispered to myself and into the earpiece.

"Okay, Auntie. I just wanted some more information regarding the mission. I know you must be busy and I'm exhausted, so I'm going to head home and get some rest," Jamie reached for her jacket.

"Alright, Jamie. We'll be in touch." Julie replied as she helped Jamie put on her jacket.

"Okay, Auntie," she responded and kissed her on the cheek.

Jamie stepped out of the house and walked to her car. She looked in my direction and I looked back at her. I stopped the recording and Jamie continued to her vehicle.

Jamie drove off and Julie began to close her door. I decided to stay behind for a few minutes before driving off so that Julie wouldn't be able to identify who I was. After about five minutes, I drove away towards Jamie's home.

***

"Ricky, am I supposed to do this mission?" Jamie asked me as we sat at her kitchen table.

"To be honest, you don't have a choice but to do it, baby," I spoke. "But the police will be prepared and well-informed, so you don't have to worry about being arrested or shot. But we only have a full day to prepare, so I will need you to spend the rest of the night and tomorrow with me so we can get you fully set up and ready."

I looked at the clock and noticed it was 3:30.

"I think we should be heading to the station, babe," I announced. "We want to catch Abel and the rest of the crew before they leave.

"Okay, Rick," Jamie spoke as she stood up.

We exited her home and entered my vehicle. I gave Abel a call once we got in the car to inform him of my new findings.

As soon as Jamie and I arrived at the station, officers rushed in and grabbed her hand. They needed to size her for a bulletproof suit. I followed behind Jamie and couldn't help but notice all the commotion going on around the office; I assume because it was because of the information I'd just provided.

I walked over to the front desk.

"Hey, Richard," Isabella stated.

"Hey, Isabella," I stated. "Pretty hectic around here, huh?"

"Yeah, ever since you called about the new drop, everyone's kind of anxious."

"Okay, Isabella. We got anything going down? Meetings or anything?" I asked her.

She looked at her notepad on her desk that was full of notes.

"Yes, sir," she replied and pointed to one of her notes. "Any and all officers who aren't occupied with Jamie or crimes, are requested to attend; especially you. Speaking of which, I was just about to head on over there."

"But you're not an officer," I joked.

"But I'm an important figure in this force," she replied. "Therefore, this is still my business."

"Yeah, yeah, yeah. You know I'm just messing with you. We couldn't do this without you," I spoke. "Let's head on over there."

Isabella locked her computer and walked from around the desk.

We walked to the meeting room and sat down. Other officers sat around the table in the room.

Abel entered the room seconds later with a cup of coffee.

"It's not too late for all that, Cap?" Jared jokingly asked.

I couldn't help but chuckle.

Abel ignored the joke and proceeded.

"Good afternoon, beautiful people."

He positioned himself behind the podium.

"We've got intel that another drop may be getting ready to go down. So, preparation is needed for a successful arrest."

Abel cleared his throat.

"Now, we lost a few men at the last drop. We can and will not have that happen this time around. Young, please come to the front," Abel finished.

I rose from my chair and approached the podium. I figured he was going to have me explain the details since I was the source of information.

He handed me a marker as I arrived at the front. "Since you have the firsthand knowledge, you're the planner with this," he chuckled.

He patted my back and walked over with his cup of coffee to where I previously sat.

"Alright, everyone, so we got a tip. What happened before is going to happen again, so we've been informed. The thing is, we can't make a move until something happens. So, we're planning this out so that we can make a successful arrest and not have any possible loopholes for the suspect to counter with a 'wrongful arrest'.

Tim raised his hand.

"Yes, Officer Charles?"

"Young, how can we be positive about this potential drop?" he asked.

"We have audio and video recording of the suspect explaining this, but, again," I spoke, "that's not enough. We're trying to catch the suspect, so something has to occur before we can make a move."

"Ah okay," he started. "Go on and finish," he added, waving me on to finish.

To begin, I explained the overall plan to burn the building down and kill many law enforcement units, but with me being the primary target.

"Why you?" Jared asserted, demonstrating to Abel there was still bad blood between us.

"I'm not sure," I calmly replied. "This is just coming straight from the recording. That's where my intel is from."

Jared started to speak again but I cut him off. I didn't want to venture off when I was supposed to be presenting.

I went down the entire timeline of how things were going to play out, and how we were going to counter everything.

Many officers agreed with my decisions, while many were skeptical.

"Guys, listen," I spoke as I concluded. "This thing is going down in two days, which doesn't give us much time. So, we all have to be on our 'A' game, okay?" I finished.

"Young, don't worry," Abel spoke as he rose to his feet. "We'll have everything together."

Abel walked back to the podium and stood beside me.

"You all heard the man," he spoke to the officers sitting down. "Get up and get moving," Abel chuckled as the officers all rose and walked out of the door.

"Officer Hubbard, can you step over here?" Abel called to Jared as he began to walk out of the room. "Close the door behind you."

Jared let out a sigh and closed the door. He walked over to Abel and me.

"I thought I made myself clear when I said I wanted for you all to squash this drama and not bring it into the workplace," Abel cleared his throat.

Jared and I were both silent.

"Now, I'm hearing reports from your fellow colleagues how they are getting a negative vibe when the two of you are together."

I put my hands in my pocket as Abel spoke.

"Now, I genuinely cannot have this behavior proceed. This is the very last time I want to see tension between the two of you in the workplace," Abel exerted. "You all don't have to shake hands and be buddy-buddy, but you damn sure better fake it while you're in here."

Jared and I looked at each other.

"Do I make myself clear?" Abel asked.

"Command received, Boss," Jared replied.

"I got you," I answered.

"Alright then," Abel finished. "Get on out of here and get to work. We got a big project coming up," he mentioned to both of us.

Jared left the room first and I left behind him.

I stepped outside to get some air. I inhaled deeply.

"Too bad it won't be fresh for long," I thought aloud.

8

"Jamie," I whispered while lightly tapping her. "Wake up, baby. It's time to start getting ready to head home. Julie may be going by there to check on you and it wouldn't look good for you not to be there."

I kissed her on the forehead and she started to wake up.

"There she is," I stated once she opened her eyes.

She looked and noticed I was fully dressed and ready: my bulletproof suit on, radio attached to my vest, my gun on my left side, handcuffs attached to my pants, my keys were in my hand and my Bluetooth attached to my ear.

"Baby, I'm worried about doing this drop. And I feel grimy for going against my aunt," Jamie told me, sitting up on the bed.

I sat down beside her and put my hand on her thigh.

"I know you don't want to work against your aunt, Jamie. But baby, you're doing the right thing. Your aunt has no reason to do what she's doing, nor should she be including you in her criminal activities." I stated.

She held her head low and I kissed her on the cheek.

She looked up at me and I kissed her on the lips.

Once I retreated, I continued to speak.

"Come on, baby," I spoke as I patted her thigh.

She let out a small sigh as she contemplated her choices.

"Okay, Ricky. Let me start getting ready. I'm going to get dressed here and then head home. Is that okay with you?" she asked.

"That's perfectly fine with me," I replied. "We just have to be sure to get you back home soon."

"Don't worry. I'll be ready," she kissed me on the cheek and walked downstairs.

When Jamie walked downstairs, I called Abel to make sure everything was prepared and ready to go.

"26th District," Isabella answered.

"Hey, Isabella, it's Richard. Is Abel around?" I asked her.

"Hey, Richard. Yes, he is. Hold on, let me transfer you."

She placed the call on hold and transferred me to his office.

"Roberts, speaking," he answered his phone.

"Roberts, it's Young. Just giving you a call to check on the status of everything. Are we good to go for today?" I asked him.

"Everything is in place. We're just waiting on the go-ahead from Jamie to move forward. We can't just have units sitting on the premises."

"You're right," I spoke. "Well, it's going down sometime tonight. I'll have to let you know the exact time momentarily. Is her suit ready?" I asked.

"It's all set," he replied. "Come on by and pick it up, Richard," I could hear him sift through some papers.

"Great. Thanks, Roberts, I'm on my way to pick it up." I hung up the phone.

I left a note on the refrigerator to notify Jamie that I would be right back.

I left my home and drove to the police station. Everyone was still in a rush over tonight's project. I walked into the building, ignoring the commotion, and walked to Abel's office.

No real conversation was passed, due to the urgency of events.

"Young, have her put this on under her clothes. We don't want for Julie to suspect *anything*," he spoke.

"I got you, Roberts," I replied before taking the suit and leaving the building.

I drove back to my home and rushed inside. Jamie heard the door close and called out.

"I'm upstairs getting dressed, babe."

"Jamie, I have your suit," I spoke as I walked upstairs. "Put it on under your clothes."

Jamie stepped outside of the room in a robe and her makeup.

"Thank you," she spoke as she kissed me on the cheek.

Her beauty was astounding to me; no way did I think she would even be capable of doing something like this on her own.

"We have a limited amount of time before we have to have you back at home." I smiled at her.

"I'll be ready in a few minutes," she stated followed by a slight wink. She then gave me a passionate kiss and reentered the room. She gently closed the door.

I pulled out my phone and checked the time. I'd also gotten a text from Abel stating that they were 100% good to go.

"Jamie, everything's right where it should be baby. Let's hope tonight goes smoothly," I spoke through the door.

"I'm sure it will be fine, baby," she answered.

Minutes later, she emerged from the room; it wasn't even possible to tell she had on the suit. Dressed in all black, she walked up to me.

"You ready, beautiful?" I asked her.

"Ready as I'll ever be," she responded.

I took her hand and we walked down the stairs. Jamie got in her vehicle and I got in mine.

Jamie drove to her home, and I drove to the airport to retrieve the helicopter.

Upon arrival, I exited and locked my vehicle. I ensured that I had my possessions and I got inside of the helicopter. I started the helicopter and flew to the police station. As I was flying, I received a text from Jamie, alerting me that Julie was at her house.

***

I flew high enough so that I wouldn't be seen by Julie or any of her crew. Tim sat in the co-pilot's chair and a few other officers sat in the back of the helicopter.

The night had fallen, and we were at the location moments before the event was to take place. I ordered the officers to turn off their lights and sirens.

They followed directions and we waited.

I spotted Jamie stepping out of the car through the helicopter's camera. "Get ready," I spoke into the radio.

I saw Jamie look around before hearing her voice over the radio.

"I hope you guys can hear me," she uttered.

She walked over to the trash can and lit the papers, and quickly got down on the ground. Once the explosion happened, the 9-1-1 call was made.

"Wait!" I stated over my radio since the officers all seemed ready to go out.

Isabella connected my phone to the audio of the call.

"Julie's on the line now," I stated over the radio.

"9-1-1, what's your emergency?" Isabella answered.

"I need police and fire trucks as soon as possible! There has been an explosion and there are flames everywhere!"

I could hear Isabella typing notes into the system.

"Mam, calm down. What is your location?" she asked Julie.

"I'm not sure exactly where I am. I was just driving around looking for my niece and I saw this happen! Please send assistance right away."

Julie sounded so believable right now, that if I didn't know any better, I would have believed her myself.

"Mam, give me a second," Isabella stated as she tried to get a location on Julie.

She muted the phone.

"No location," Isabella spoke over the radio.

"Son of a bitch is on a burner," I spoke in disgust.

"I'm getting a ping off of multiple cell towers," she spoke over the radio. "There's no accurate depiction."

Isabella unmuted the call.

"Mam, please do me a favor. I need to know where you are so that I can send emergency personnel to your location. I would like for you to hang up and call me right back," Isabella told Julie.

Julie disconnected from the call and minutes started to pass.

"Young, she's running a little late," Abel stated over his radio.

"Impossible," I added. "She's never late."

"Ricky, where are you?" Jamie whispered into the earpiece. "Time is winding down and I'm not trying to blow up with these explosives," Jamie chuckled, yet was nervous.

"We're waiting on your aunt to call back, Jamie," I spoke.

A thought quickly came to mind as I finished speaking to Jamie.

"Julie's smarter than this, Roberts," I stated on my radio.

"What do you mean?" he asked.

"Julie knows that if she calls back, we will get her exact location and that will be the end of this. I'm sending a transmission to Isabella and having her forcibly call the number back and pull an exact location."

"10-4. I will radio for a fire truck now," Abel spoke. "We're sending our men out. We can't hold off, any longer."

"Ricky, hurry," Jamie spoke as the flames started to surround her and block off her exits, barricading her on the top of the building.

I sent a transmission over the radio to Isabella.

"Isabella, I need for you to force a call back to Julie's number and pull a location! Also, check into the national 9-1-1 security database and tell me if Julie has somehow gotten routed there."

I could hear Isabella working quickly.

"She's just hung up with the national 9-1-1 network. For some reason, the call wasn't routed to us."

"Julie's such a smartass," I spoke out of disgust. "You guys, get ready to deploy," I announced to the officers in the helicopter.

I started to lower the aircraft.

"Calling her number back, now!" Isabella spoke as the firetrucks arrived on the scene and the ground officers emerged from their vehicles.

The SWAT team unloaded from their vans and started to run up the stairs.

"Jamie, get the hell out of there," I spoke over the radio. "SWAT team, hold your fire and positions."

"I got it, Richard!" Isabella exclaimed. "I'm sending the location to Abel's GPS unit right now."

"Thank you, Isabella," I stated as I got out of the helicopter and drew my weapon. "Roberts, send that location to my phone."

Tim and the rest of the officers emerged from the helicopter before I took the lead.

I quickly ran up the stairs and I passed the SWAT team who were waiting.

"Go back down, get into position," I shouted to the SWAT team members.

I continued up the stairs, regardless of the heat and I bumped into Jamie who was coming down the stairs.

"Ricky, I can't do this," Jamie cried to me.

"Jamie, *we* can do this," I assured her.

I gave her a quick kiss as another explosion occurred at the top of the building.

"Baby, go!" I told her.

She continued to run downstairs. As I reached the top, I was almost burned due to the amount of heat.

"Top of the building is destroyed," I spoke over the radio. "I do not have a vantage point from here. Proceed with the rest of the plan; shoot the man's tires," I shouted as I ran back downstairs.

The snipers in the helicopter above shot out the man's tires, as he gave Jamie the explosive.

Many officers ran in and arrested the guy on the motorcycle as he attempted to ride off.

"Disabling the elevator now!" Isabella stated over the radio.

I arrived downstairs and I reached Jamie as she briefly pulled one of the smaller explosives off.

"Disable this, Ricky," she panicked as she ran and stuck the explosives on the corners of the building and she placed the primary bomb inside the elevator.

Since Isabella disabled them, the elevator wouldn't travel up the building. The doors remained open.

One of Julie's suspects ran up and pushed Jamie back into me, before running off.

"What the fuck?" I muttered as Jamie ran off to follow her aunt's direction.

"From the heat on the 24th floor, there's absolutely no way anyone can be alive up there!" Abel shouted on the radio.

"Richard, you have a vehicle coming at you, doing about 120 miles per hour. It's about 3 miles away," Isabella mentioned. "I am trying to work as fast as I can with the specialist right now, but he's telling me that he physically needs be on-site to work."

"What about the other specialists?" I stated as Jamie hid in the non-working elevator.

"They aren't trained for these explosives," Isabella spoke.

"Who the fuck would send out these untrained specialists?" I asked. "Roberts, abort this mission. Arrest suspects and get the hell out of here," I spoke. "I have to try to disable this bomb, myself."

"Young, we are not leaving you here by yourself," he shouted. "Stick to the plan."

I lowered my radio's volume and got on my knees. About 2 minutes were remaining on the explosives on the ground of the building.

I stripped the coat of the wire, so I could see the metal that was used.

Jamie continued to hide and Jared pulled up beside me with Madeline in the front seat.

There was another explosion on many floors of the building. Glass started to fall, as well as wood, chipped bricks, and office supplies.

"Richard, get in," Jared shouted.

"No, not until I finish with this explosive!" I retaliated.

The timer was now at 45 seconds.

"Shit, shit, shit," I spoke.

"So, you're willing to die over catching Julie?" he asked.

I ignored him and pulled out the pocket-knife I possessed.

I held the wires to the bomb and briefly tied them together, leaving a knot in the middle. I quickly cut the red wire and the timer on the explosive stopped with only a few seconds remaining.

"Jamie, come here," I shouted. "Stay hidden right here in this elevator; do not leave this spot. I am going for your aunt," I added.

I gave Jamie a quick kiss before speaking over my radio. "Area secured," I mentioned over my radio. "I have defused the bomb and am going after Julie."

"We're going to have to request backup, Richard," Abel spoke. "Hold tight."

"I'm going for Julie," I spoke. "She's not getting away."

I got in Jared's car and he continued to drive straight towards Julie's location, according to the location information Isabella pulled.

"Madeline I'm going to need your help," I told her.

"What's up?" she asked.

"We're going to get Julie. Me and you," I told her.

As Jared drove, the more I could hear helicopters arriving and sirens approaching. Jared got to the location a mile later, and I saw someone standing on the top.

"Julie," I thought aloud.

"Rick, are you sure you and Madeline can handle Julie?" Jared asked me.

"Yea, don't worry your pretty little heart about it!" I told him and got out of the backseat.

Madeline got out of the front and Jared drove off.

I spoke to Madeline.

"Madeline, no matter what happens, stay focused. Do not let your girly side get to you," I chuckled.

"Richard, please. You know I'm tougher than you," she laughed.

I laughed before proceeding.

"Let's go." I pulled out my gun and we both walked over to the character.

"Julie Wilson, stand up and put your hands in the air," I projected.

Julie was sitting comfortably in a lawn chair, looking at the chaos and mayhem below. She held a Cuban cigar in her hand.

"Richard, you may want to take two steps to the right and one step forward," she stated, not once looking back at myself or Madeline.

"Julie, rise to your feet," I reinforced.

Madeline and I didn't want to get too close because we didn't know what lurked behind Julie.

"Slowly," Madeline added.

A stray bullet whizzed past my ear.

"I told you to move over," Julie stated with a chuckle and slowly rose to her feet with her hands up. "How nice to see you, what brings you here today?" she asked me. "It's pretty crazy over here."

"Julie, you are under arrest," Madeline spoke moving closer to her.

"Under arrest?" Julie questioned. "I don't feel like I'm under arrest," she finished.

"Just wait on it," I spoke. "It'll kick in."

"What am I under arrest for?" she asked. "I have a right to know."

"Julie, are we looking at the same thing?" Madeline asked. "It's a riot down there, and you dare ask such a question?"

"I haven't done a thing, nor do I appreciate you accusing me of it," Julie retaliated.

"Yeah, right," I spoke, never taking my eyes off Julie.

Julie let out a sigh.

"Alright, it's clear you're not going to believe me. So, come on, just arrest me." Julie told me.

"Turn around Julie," I told her as she faced me.

She turned around and allowed me to begin to put the handcuffs on her. Immediately with her free hand, she jerked, turned around, and gave me a violent shove to the ground. As soon as she pushed me, Julie broke out into a run.

Madeline aimed her gun at Julie and then stopped and kneeled to tend to me.

"I'm good, Madeline," I stated holding my chest.

With the shove, the wind was knocked out of me.

A car came speeding and halted for Julie to get in before speeding off.

"No plates," I spoke in disgust.

I looked to the crowd and saw that some of the suspects were now shooting at the police officers.

Multiple helicopters arrived on the scene; officers were shooting out of the side of the aircraft.

"It's a mess down there, Madeline," I told her, only to be interrupted by my cell phone.

I answered and was shocked to hear Julie on the line.

"Richard, I do not want to hear your words. I know you had outside help and when I get my hands on them, you can kiss them goodbye; but I already know who it is, seeing as though I've only let one other person besides Linda know," Julie emitted a small laugh. "And I don't think Linda was of any help to you," she finished and hung up.

Madeline helped me rise to my feet.

"Roberts, mission failed. Julie has assaulted me and is on the run," I spoke over my radio.

Several backup officers arrived on the premises, while some of the suspects got into their vehicles and drove away. Madeline and I both walked back towards my helicopter.

The walk was silent for the most part. We still heard helicopters overhead, but overall, it was quiet because many of the suspects were apprehended. Firemen were also arriving on the scene to put out the flames.

We were almost to my helicopter when I saw one of the gunmen walking with Jamie.

"Walk faster!" he yelled to her.

Madeline and I immediately took cover by a nearby car.

Madeline and I each drew our weapons and aimed them at the man holding Jamie hostage.

"Jamie," I shouted to get the gunman's attention, as well as Jamie's.

The gunman turned around and aimed his gun at Jamie's head.

"Drop your weapon," I stated with my gun aimed.

"You better listen to him," Madeline warned.

I slightly moved my finger to ensure that the safety mechanism was disabled.

He didn't verbally respond to me. He put his finger on the trigger and started to squeeze.

I didn't even give him the opportunity. In an instant, I shot him in the forehead, right between the eyes. The gunman instantly fell to the ground, releasing his hold on Jamie.

I held my weapon securely in my hand as I walked over to Jamie and the man. Upon arriving at Jamie, I holstered my weapon and hugged her tightly.

Madeline walked over to the man and put her fingers on his neck to try to feel a pulse; there was none.

"We need an ambulance over here at 320 East Erie. Suspect down," Madeline stated over her radio.

I continued to hug Jamie as tears accumulated in her eyes.

"He's dead," Madeline spoke. She quickly turned the situation around to be my fault. "You couldn't shoot him in the leg?" she argumentatively asked.

"He posed an immediate threat! I had to take charge." I retaliated.

"You could have quickly tried to deescalate the situation. Talk him out of it," Madeline explained.

"And then what?" I asked. "The man was pressing down on the trigger and was going to kill Jamie."

Madeline shook her head.

"You could have talked him out of it," she reiterated. "Plus, if he wanted to kill her, he would have done so."

"This conversation is pointless," I spoke. "I don't understand what you aren't comprehending right now," I shook my head. "He posed a threat to our character witness." "Jamie?" Madeline questioned. "News flash," Madeline added. "With or without Jamie, this case would be going on."

"Nah, it wouldn't," I stated calmly. "Julie needed Jamie to pull this off. And although she's fresh out and says she doesn't want criminal activity tracing back to her name, she sure does have a weird way of showing it by shoving me to the ground."

Jamie was truly speechless at everything, but she wanted to speak. She fixed her mouth to say something, but the words wouldn't come out. She hugged me tighter.

"Yes, Julie assaulted you. I give you that. But you and I both know she's smarter than that. She's going to do her best to stay off of our radar, so what makes you think she would send someone to kill her niece? And even so, that does not mean to kill a suspect; where's our case at now? You know you're supposed to aim low!" Madeline shouted.

More news helicopters were hovering over us and were broadcasting what was happening.
"He posed a threat to the key to this whole case!" I shouted to Madeline.
"Aim for the leg, why shoot him in his forehead?" Madeline yelled.
"Oh yeah, I aim for the leg and he aims for the head. He needs crutches while we're making funeral arrangements for Jamie," I spoke sarcastically.

Madeline let out a sigh and proceeded to speak again.
"So, what do we tell the paramedics once they arrive?" she calmly asked.
"I'm just going to tell them what happened," I told her. "The whole truth."
"As long as you have your story in order," Madeline spoke. "Oh, and Ricky, all I'm going to say is this: you handled the situation with Madison and Jared all wrong. You pulled a gun out on him. Jared's been your boy for too long."
"Madeline, I don't want to talk about this right now," I told her as I shook my head.
"Soon enough you are going to have to," Madeline stated and sharply stopped herself.
"What do you mean?" I asked her, confused as to why she said what she said.
"Nothing Rich," she replied shaking her head.
Seeing that she wasn't going to give in, I took Jamie's hand and walked over to the helicopter.

I helped Jamie in the backseat and Madeline into the passenger side. An ambulance arrived as I helped the two inside.
"Detective!" The paramedic called and waved over to me.
"I'm not sure of his name, but he's been down for about five minutes," I announced as I walked over to him.
The paramedic jotted down the notes, as his teammates put the man on a stretcher.

"We're pronouncing him DOA," the paramedic spoke, "but if we get him back and can sustain a pulse, we will let you know."

"Well, here's my card," I told him as I handed him a card.

I walked back to the helicopter and climbed inside.

The ambulance left the scene with the man in the back of the vehicle. I had a feeling they wouldn't be contacting me regarding him being alive.

A few officers remained on the scene with the firefighters; since I'd gotten clearance from Abel, I decided it was time for us to leave.

"You all ready?" I asked Jamie and Madeline as I ensured the doors were locked.

"Yes," they both responded in unison.

I raised the helicopter and proceeded to fly to the airport when I received a text message. I put the helicopter on auto-pilot and read the message; it was from Madeline. Letter by letter I continued to read the message:

'Madison is pregnant.'

I dropped my phone to the floor of the helicopter and I sat there; Madeline could tell I read the message. She put her hand on my shoulder and I grabbed the navigation mechanism and disengaged the auto-pilot.

The rest of the flight to retrieve my vehicle was silent.

9

When I arrived home, I assisted Jamie in getting out of the vehicle. I then walked over to Madeline's side and waited a few seconds before speaking.

"Jamie, go in the house. I'll be right there," I told her.

Jamie walked into the house and I started to talk to Madeline.

"Madeline, is what you texted me true?" I asked her, praying that she said no.

"Madison is two months pregnant, and she thinks the baby may be yours," Madeline reiterated.

"But who's to say? How long has she been messing around with Jared? No one knows. She could have been doing it for a long time now," I told Madeline, desperately trying to mentally escape.

I honestly didn't want to feel like being trapped in a commitment with Madison after she did what she did.

"Rick, you have to accept this. Madison may be carrying your child and if she is, you need to support her and the baby. If you aren't going to be there for her, you need to at least be there for the child," Madeline sounded as though she were my mother.

I let out a deep sigh and continued. "So, what do you suggest I do?"

"Well, for one, you need to call Madison and Jared so that you all can sit down and talk about it. That's step one; it will answer many questions."

"You're right, Madeline. I'll give Madison and Jared a call tomorrow," I spoke. "But how will I tell Jamie?"

"I don't have all the answers, Rick," Madeline stated, "you have to figure that one out," she chuckled.

I embraced Madeline before we both walked into the home.

"Jamie," I called out.

She emerged from the sitting room and came into the living room.

"Yes, Ricky?" she stated as she sat beside me.

Her sweet smile and innocent face made the moment even more difficult.

I took her hands in mine.

"Jamie, you know I care about you, but I have to tell you something that may affect what we have going on."

Jamie had an inquisitive look on her face.

"What do you mean?" she asked.

I took a deep breath before proceeding.

"You know Madison, right?" I asked her.

"Yes. What about her?" Jamie asked me.

"Well," I started and let out a sigh. "She's..." I started.

As I was about to continue speaking, a vision came to me.

"Hit the deck!" I shouted as I pulled out my gun.

Madeline got on the floor, but Jamie, who didn't know about this feature I had, remained propped up on the chair.

"Jamie, get down," Madeline shouted.

As Jamie got down beside Madeline, Molotov cocktails came in through the windows. A total of four cocktails broke the windows. One by one, they each hit the floor and the curtains. The room was soon in flames.

"Come on, ladies," I spoke to Jamie and Madeline.

We all crawled to the door and I reached up to open it. Jamie and Madeline rose to their feet before running outside. I stepped outside and looked at my home in disgust; I already had an idea as to whom was responsible.

I spoke on my radio, informing officers that I would need a fire truck to my house, as well as some backup.

The whole house was soon ignited. We all stood outside the home waiting for assistance. As each minute passed, it felt as though the temperature was dropping.

"I guess we better be grateful that we could get out. If we couldn't we'd all be dead," I stated aloud.

I never took my eyes from the home, but I heard a car pull up.

Jared got out of the car and walked up to me.

"What happened here?" he asked while snickering.

"This shit ain't funny!" I told him. "Where are those trucks at?".

"They're on their way," Jared spoke as Madison got out of the car.

I shook my head and turned around. I walked over to Madison as she stood by the car.

"I hear you're pregnant," I told her. "And you believe it's mine."

Madison tried to avoid eye contact with me.

"Yes, the baby may be yours," she stated.

An unidentifiable car drove by the house, noticed the commotion taking place, and drove off.

"Madison, why did you mess around? Didn't I give you everything you ever wanted?" I asked her.

I was hoping to get answers to something that had been troubling me this entire time.

"It wasn't that Ricky, but you were always busy with work and didn't really have any time for me."

"Madison, don't hit me with that B.S. You knew what I did when we first met! You most definitely cannot use that against me." I looked up and noticed Linda passing by and I became suspicious. "Jared, be ready," I called to him.

"Well Ricky, you really shouldn't worry. We only made love a few times; while I believe this baby may be yours, I have a strong feeling that it's Jared's."

"Madison, are you kidding me?!" I chuckled in disbelief. "You've been messing with Jared this whole time, huh?"

Madison got frightened and started backing away and I turned away from her to catch my breath.

Madison walked towards the curb, not knowing what to say and unaware Madeline followed her.

The car pulled up again. This time, it briefly pulled over.

Julie grabbed Madison and forced her into the car.

"Richard!" Madeline yelled and started to attack Julie, but had very little success.

Julie knocked Madeline to the ground and drove off.

I immediately turned around and ran over to her, along with Jamie and Jared.

"Julie has Madison! She came by and forced her in the car!" Madeline shouted.

"Shit," I spoke in disgust.

I helped Madeline up, acknowledging her wounds.

"Jamie, go get my car and pull it around to the front," I shouted to her.

Jared got in his vehicle and sped in the direction that Julie traveled.

Once Jamie drove around, she and I helped Madeline get in the car.

"Madeline, we need to get you to a hospital," I told her.

I observed the deep cut on her face.

"I don't need to go to a hospital. All I need are a couple of bandages and to save my four-month pregnant friend."

"Four months?" I asked her. "I thought you said two."

"That was because I wanted to see how you would react to me saying that she was pregnant."

The more she spoke, the angrier I got.

"Fuck it, let's go," I shook my head. "And when this is all over, I'm through with you and Jared," I spoke to Madeline.

"Richard..." she started, disappointedly.

I ignored her and positioned myself in the seat to drive.

"Everyone buckle up," Jamie stated, knowing we were about to speed.

She kissed me on the cheek and put on her seatbelt. I looked at my burning house before driving off.

"Un-fucking-believable," I stated and turned on my police radio.

"Calling all officers, we have a hostage situation, in pursuit of a blue Chevy Corvette. Officer Hubbard, radio in with the details of their location."

I released the microphone button and Jared quickly chimed in.

"Suspect is in a green Pontiac, heading west on 290."

"Which one is it? Blue Chevy or green Pontiac?" Abel asked, confused.

"Green Pontiac, 2011" Jared answered.

"10-4. Cars and choppers are en route."

I firmly gripped the steering wheel and watched as my speedometer crept up towards the maximum speed of 160 miles-per-hour.

"Ricky... I'm sorry." Madeline stated, interrupting my thoughts.

I didn't reply to her, verbally, but she could tell I was listening to what she was saying.

"Yes. I'm sorry for lying to you," she continued. "I'm sorry for even letting you get mixed in with my best friend," she had tears in her eyes. "As your fellow law enforcement partner, I shouldn't have allowed it to happen. I'm sorry for everything." Madeline finished.

I didn't respond. I continued to speed to catch up with Jared and Julie. In a matter of seconds, I saw the other police vehicles and sped past them. I switched gears and drove side-by-side with Julie.

She looked to her left and saw me; she immediately hit her brakes, causing the other officers and myself to swerve to avoid hitting her.

Many of the officers swerved into the lanes of traffic flowing in the opposite direction and collided with some of the other vehicles.

Julie briefly pulled over, pushed Madison out of the car, and sped off.

Many of the cars traveling on the expressway quickly hit their brakes to avoid hitting any of us. Many of the officers set a roadblock and started to direct traffic off of the expressway.

I quickly pulled over and ran towards Madison; Jared, Madeline, and Jamie followed me. I kneeled, put one hand on Madison's stomach and the other on her face, and I wiped the tears from her eyes.

"Watch out, Richard," Jared shouted as he shoved me out of the way.

Julie had driven away, and all of the other officers stopped once Madison was thrown out of the car. My first thought was that they'd stopped because Madison was obtained, but I quickly realized that they'd stopped because Jared and I stopped the pursuit.

As Jared shoved me, my first instinct was to attack him, but I didn't want to create additional drama, so I decided to walk back over to Madison, who was still on the ground and crying.

"Come on Madison," I stated, helping her up, with Jared holding her other hand.

Madison jerked away from Jared and rested her head on my shoulder. I walked over to my car and sat Madison on the hood. I took off my jacket and put it around her. I sat down beside her, and she rested her head on my shoulder, once more.

Additional officers began to swarm in and surround us.

"Are you okay, Madison?" I asked her while ignoring the other officers.

Abel exited his vehicle after typing notes into his system and walked over towards us.

She was holding her stomach with one hand and holding the jacket with the other. Jared jogged over to myself and Madison, and I tapped her to lift her head to avoid confrontation with him.

I stood up and backed away; Jared kissed her.

"Baby, are you okay?" he asked her and noticed she was holding her stomach. "Did she do something to my little man?" He kneeled.

"I'm fine baby, my stomach just hurts," Madison wiped her eyes. "She just put me in the car and sped. She wanted to hold me for ransom and tried to get out of view as soon as she grabbed me. Then, she noticed all of the police cars behind us. That's when she decided to put me out," she explained. "She was gonna kill me and the baby, even after she got the ransom money." Madison started to cry harder.

Jared helped her off of the car and put her into his car. He removed my jacket from Madison and threw it out of the vehicle.

I glared at Jared while Jamie kneeled to pick it up.

This sign of disrespect was the final straw.

"No baby, leave it," I told her. "Jared, get your punk ass over here and pick up my jacket!" I shouted to him.

Other officers started to watch as they remembered our previous encounter.

Jared looked to Abel for verification.

"Gentlemen, this is ridiculous," Abel spoke. "Jared, please go retrieve the jacket."

I rolled my eyes at Abel's comment. Jamie rose to her feet and stood beside me.

Jared approached me, and I whispered under my breath. I took off my bulletproof vest, as well as my keys, my gun, and my cell phone. Jared kept his hand on his gun and kneeled in front of me to pick up the jacket.

"Baby, don't do it," Jamie whispered to me, kissing me on the cheek. Jared handed me the jacket and stood there facing me. I turned around, but continued to watch from the corner of my eye; as soon as I saw Jared's hand leave his gun, I swung my fist and hit him in the face; the impact knocked him to the ground.

He got on his hands and knees and attempted to get up but I repeatedly kicked him in his stomach, although he was coughing up blood.

Madison stepped out of the car and other officers started to run in, including Abel, while Jamie tried to hold me back. I ripped free from her hold and kneeled down and repeatedly punched Jared, causing his nose to bleed.

He continued to cough up blood and it took several officers to pull me off of him. When they finally got me off Jared, his mouth was full of blood and his nose was bleeding.

"Baby," Jamie stated and started to cry.

At this moment, all of the officers knew something was going on between Jamie and me.

I pulled her close and kissed her on the forehead, still glaring at Jared. He stared at me and held his stomach. I picked up my things in one of my hands, took Jamie's hand in my other, and walked her to the car.

"Detective, I need to have a word with you," Abel spoke.

"Later, Cap," I spoke as I got into my vehicle.

I started the car and drove off, leaving Jared, Madison, and the other officers in disbelief.

10

No words were spoken for the entire drive.

"Madeline," I finally spoke as she got out of the vehicle.

She turned around but didn't say anything.

"We'll discuss the thing about Madison and Jared later," I spoke.

"Have a good night, Richard," she spoke to me. "You too, Jamie," she closed the door.

Jamie raised a hand to wave back to Madeline.

I watched Madeline inside of her home before driving off.

I drove in the direction of Jamie's home and prepared myself to merge onto the expressway.

"Richard," Jamie spoke softly, "take me with you. I just want to make sure you're alright."

I wasn't in the mood to debate, so I let out a sigh and changed my destination to return to my home.

Firemen and police officers were all around the building. I pulled out my badge.

"Jamie, stay here for a minute. Lock the doors and sit tight. I'll be right back," I told her.

"Okay, Ricky," she stated. "But I'm drinking this water," she chuckled as she held the water bottle that resided in the cupholder.

"I'm not about to play with you," I laughed as I closed the door.

I walked up to the officers and firemen.

"Are you the owner of this unit?" An officer asked as he referenced the burned building.

"Yes, I am. But I'm legitimately trying to figure out where you all were about an hour ago," I chuckled in disgust. "It's sad. Being a cop doesn't even get you a decent sense of protection," I raised my tone.

"Sir, I'm going to need for you to calm down." The same officer responded.

I took in a deep breath.

"Now what? In terms of my house." I asked him.

"Our men will call in sanitation for cleanup, so don't worry about the mess. Just go around and if you see anything you need, go on and grab it. Being part of the force, I'm sure you have insurance, am I right?"

"Of course," I told him, offended and annoyed with his sarcasm.

"Well," he started, "take this card and give these people a call. Once you get in touch with him, they'll have someone come out to look at the mess and go from there. So we'll wait to have it cleaned up. We'll just leave tape up."

I took the card from the officer and walked over to the charred rubble of what used to be my home.

Each step I took resulted in the crunching and crackling sound of the mess. The only thing that survived the fire was my safe and it was unmoved.

I walked over to my safe and kneeled. I typed in my code, slowly opened the door, finding exactly 3 straps of one-hundred-dollar bills, and a photo of Jamie and myself that we had taken months prior.

I grabbed the money and the picture and walked back over to the car.

"What happened, Ricky?" Jamie asked me as I got in the car.

She held the empty water bottle in her hand.

"I have to call the insurance company," I told her as I put my car into gear; I kept my foot on the brake.

"What's that?" she asked me as she noticed the picture.

I held the picture at an angle that she could view it.

"Ricky, this is when we first started to date," Jamie spoke as tears accumulated in her eyes.

"It is," I chuckled. "Listen, Jamie: over these past few months, I've developed feelings for you. I don't tell this to just anyone, but I love you," I told her.

"I love you, too, Ricky," she replied while trying her best not to cry.

I held Jamie's hand in my right hand and I kept the left hand on the steering wheel.

I drove until I reached the Plaza Galleria hotel. I could have gone to Jamie's home, but that would be the most obvious place for Julie to catch us together.

Jamie and I got out of the car and we entered the building.

Jamie took a seat on the bench as I approached the service desk. I explained my situation and got a room to stay in.

Jamie and I took the elevator to the 12th floor and proceeded to walk to the room.

Once we got settled into the room, I took Jamie's hand in mine.

"You ready baby?" I asked her.

"Will you tell me where we're going, Ricky?" Jamie asked me.

"You still asking questions, baby?" I chuckled and kissed her on the cheek.

We left the lights on and walked out of the room.
***

I unlocked the door and I entered after Jamie, carrying many bags of various items, including clothing, jewelry, shoes, and purses.

"This was so much fun, Richard," Jamie stated with a laugh.

"Anything for you, baby," I told her, placing the bags down.

Jamie walked to the bathroom and I decided to pull out the room service menu.

"Baby, you want anything from downstairs?" I called to her.

"No, babe," Jamie stated. "I'll be out in a few," she answered.

I picked up the phone and called downstairs.

"Room service," the woman answered.

"Hey, can you all bring up a bottle of your finest champagne and two wine glasses?" I asked her.

"A bottle of champagne and two wine glasses, is there anything else, Mr. Young?"

"No mam, that is all," I replied.

"Okay," she spoke. "We will have it up in about three minutes," she finished.

"Thank you," I told her, hanging up the phone.

As I hung up the phone, Jamie called to me. I walked over to the bathroom door.

"Hey babe, what's your favorite color?" she asked.

"Blue, baby... sometimes a red and black combination. Why?" I asked.

"No reason," I could tell she was smiling. "I'll be out in a minute baby," Jamie stated.

I didn't want Jamie to know what I had ordered, so I stepped outside to prevent room service from knocking. I stepped one foot outside and looked down the hall.

I saw the man coming down the hall with a tray. On the tray sat the two wine glasses and the bottle of champagne. He was dressed in an all-white suit with diamond cufflinks; he seemed as if he could be the owner of the hotel and not just kitchen help.

"Here you go, Mr. Young: your wine, as well as your wine glasses." He handed me the tray.

"Thank you, my good man," I told him as I handed him a fifty-dollar bill.

"Thank you. If you need anything else, don't hesitate to call back down," he replied before turning around and walking off.

I returned to the room and I put the bottle of Merlot in the ice bucket beside the two glasses. I filled the glasses half-way and turned back around.

Jamie stood there wearing a two-piece black and red lingerie outfit with high heels. She approached me and swung her hips with every step. Jamie reached me and put her hands on my chest, slowly working them up to remove my jacket.

"I'm assuming those hips don't lie," I chuckled. "Baby, what's all this?" I asked her with a smile.

"There will be no stressing tonight," Jamie replied seductively, raising her wine glass and taking a sip. After she took a sip, she raised the glass to my lips.

After I took a sip, she put her wine glass down and removed my jacket while kissing me passionately. I dropped my jacket onto the floor and removed my shirt.

I continued to kiss Jamie as I put my hands on her soft shoulders. I ran one of my hands through her curly brown hair and I used my other hand to undo the top strap to her lingerie piece.

"Rick," Jamie stated to me.

"Yes, baby?" I responded as I kissed her neck.

"I love you," she answered softly.

"I love you, too, Jamie," I responded.

"But I'm not ready to have any babies." Jamie finished.

"I got you," I told her.

I listened to her let out moans of pleasure as I kissed her and ran my hands down her body.

She wrapped her hands around my neck and she jumped on me, wrapping her legs around my waist.

"Come on, Daddy," she moaned as she started to scratch my back while I gently sucked and kissed on her neck.

I held her tightly and grabbed her thigh as I laid her down on the bed. I continued to kiss down her body and I caressed every inch of her soft skin.

I returned to her face, kissed her lips, and she let out a slight moan of satisfaction as she started to breathe heavily in my ear. Between every movement that I made, she let out heavier moans and they slowly erupted into gentle, audible, and erotic screams of pleasure.

I ran my fingers through her hair as she continued to scratch my back and I could feel myself starting to drown in her ocean.

Although she didn't tell me, I could tell that this was her first time. As Jamie and I made love, we had no idea that we were being watched.

***

We were both lying down in the bed, surrounded by our sweat, passion, and love.

Jamie's head rested on my chest and I ran my fingers through her hair.

"Baby, what's going on with Madison?" Jamie asked me.

I let out a sigh and held Jamie's hand.

"Jamie, Madison's four months pregnant, and she thinks it may be mine," I answered.

Immediately, I could see a change in her attitude, as she lifted her head from my chest.

"Well, what do *you* think?" she asked me.

"Baby, I don't know what to think. I don't believe it's mine, because she was messing around with Jared behind my back," I started, "and I'm not sure how long that's been going on. I guess we won't know until the baby comes," I shrugged.

"What if the baby is yours, Ricky?" Jamie asked me; I could tell she was nervous to ask.

"If it's mine," I held her hand tighter, "I will support the baby, but me and her are through. I'm here for you, Jamie," I assured her.

I laid a kiss on her lips.

Jamie retreated from the kiss and stood up. Wearing nothing but a towel, she walked over to the bags that we had bought and pulled out one that I hadn't seen before. Inside of the bag were two small black cases.

"Richard, I love you. And I want you to promise me that you're here for me." Jamie stated and opened the cases.

Inside were matching rings, a male and female. Jamie placed the ring on my finger and kissed my cheek.

"Promise me" she stated.

I thought for a second before speaking.

"Close your eyes, Jamie," I stated.

She was curious as to why I asked her to close her eyes, but she did it anyway, and I walked over to the bags. I pulled out another bag with a longer jewelry case.

I pulled out a necklace. It was long, white-gold, and covered with 6 karat diamonds, at least ten of them. In the middle of the necklace lied a tiny .25 karat diamond with a picture of

Jamie and me, with the words, 'Richard and Jamie forever' embedded.

I carefully held the jewel and walked it over to Jamie. I positioned myself behind her and put the necklace around her neck. I fastened the latch and let the necklace hang.

"Open your eyes, Jamie," I stated with my hands on her shoulders.

She opened her eyes and looked down to find the necklace dangling and my hands on her shoulders.

"I promise," I whispered to Jamie and I kissed her neck again.

"Baby, what...?" Jamie started.

"Baby, look right here," I stated as I pointed to the heart in the middle, "this heart represents my heart, and this," I pointed to the diamonds inside of the heart, "represents our love. The diamonds surrounding it represent the outside temptations that try to destroy what we have." I told Jamie before I kissed her on the neck. "Jamie, I love you and will do anything in my power to make sure you are safe and happy," I told her.

"I'm speechless, Richard," Jamie stated.

"Don't say anything then, baby," I told her and kissed her again.

I put my arm around Jamie and we lied back down. Soon, we were both asleep.

11

The next morning, I showered and decided to check my email before Jamie woke up.

I walked over to my laptop and logged in. An alert popped up, letting me know that I had 26 new messages, mostly from other officers and one regarding today's assignment.

Right above the email for today's assignment was an email that appeared to be spam at first sight until I saw Jamie's name and it arrived at the precise time I logged on.

I looked over to Jamie; she was still asleep.

I opened the email and began to read it.

Dear Richard Young,
I'm assuming that's how you start an email... All of my other emails aren't formal. Anyway, I am writing to you on behalf of what happened last night. It is so fucking unfortunate that Jamie got tied up with you! To think that blood is thicker than water; you're the reason I was locked away for years.
And what went down with Officer Hubbard? I mean, really, who fights their best friend over a girl? But thank you, because you have let me know to never attempt to take you on. If I was him, my ass would be dead...

I stopped reading the email as I heard Jamie waking up.

I walked over to her and kneeled at the bedside. I ran my fingers up and down her cheek. Jamie opened her eyes and I was the first thing she saw.

"Hey, beautiful," I stated before I kissed her on the cheek.

"Hey Ricky," Jamie stated and looked down.

I was still wearing the ring and she was still wearing the necklace. Jamie smiled but continued to lie down. "Baby, what are you doing?" she asked as I walked back over to my computer.

"I got an email, baby and I'm trying to see what it's about." I didn't want to let Jamie know the details of the email yet.

"Baby, you're always caught up in your work," Jamie stated with a chuckle.

"That's because I'm a busy person, baby," I chuckled. I continued to read the email.

...But then again, I wouldn't be, cause I'm always a step ahead of you. Oh, and congrats on the future Lil Ricky. Yea, I heard Madison was pregnant, so I let the bitch go. I wasn't even gonna deal with that...

With every word I read, the angrier I got. I knew this was from Julie, and I didn't want to rest until she was caught.

How's Jamie? Did you all enjoy yourselves last night? Yup, Linda informed me that she saw y'all all hugged up and whatnot. Such a two-dollar hoe. How is Jamie gonna turn her back on family for a worthless piece of shit like you? I shoulda known that bitch was wearing a wire when she made that unexpected arrival. Pathetic hoe. But it's cool. When the time is right, she'll come back. Until then, just know I am always watching. I know you are in the Plaza Galleria hotel, room 1248, and you probably have this stupid look on your face as you're wondering how I know this lol. Anyway. I have to go. TTYS!

I was super angry and walked over to Jamie.

"What's wrong baby?" Jamie asked me.

"Your aunt, she knows where we are. I don't know how, but she can see us. The email was from her." I told her, gripping my holster with my gun inside.

"What did she say?" Jamie asked, slightly frightened.

"I'm gonna let you read it, baby."

I let Jamie read the email and I could see the fear in her eyes as she finished. I reached out and hugged her.

"This is all my fault, Ricky," Jamie stated as she shook her head.

"No, it's not, Jamie," I assured her. "No one is at fault but Julie herself," I confirmed. I continued to look around, suspicious of a potential camera in the room.

"We need to get out of here. There is no telling what Julie will try since she knows where we are."

"So, what do we do now?"

"Well, first Jamie, we need to leave this hotel room ASAP. And then, we take it from there," I spoke. "We need to be where we aren't accessible to your aunt. If your aunt can see us, she may try anything at any given time, not only in the night." I had to think.

I could use my sixth sense, but Jamie wouldn't know anything about it, so I had to tell her.

"Come here, baby," I stated.

Jamie walked over to where I'd relocated, and I started to tell her. I told her all about my sixth sense and how I realized I had it and how it worked.

"So, last night, when you told me and Madeline to get down, it was your —..."

"Sixth sense," I finished her sentence. "Yes, baby. And it really comes in handy at times."

Jamie walked over to the hotel window and I walked over and stood next to her.

"Ricky, if you really have a sixth sense, why don't you use it?" Jamie asked me.

I could tell she was confused at how it worked with me.

"I can use it, baby, but it's not like an 'on-demand' thing. Sometimes, it just happens. Really happens for big events," I replied. I looked out the window. "Your aunt is somewhere out there, but I assure you, she cannot do anything, baby." I kissed her on the cheek. "I'm right here."

Jamie kissed me on the cheek and walked to the washroom to take a shower.

I opened my assignment emails, put many of them on hold, and reassigned a few that required immediate attention. Walking back over to the window, I took a good look. In the distance, I saw someone looking in my direction.

"Julie" I mumbled under my breath.

I closed the blinds and walked back to my computer when the phone rang. I walked over and answered the phone.

"Is everything okay, Richard?" Julie spoke over the phone.

"Julie, I swear, when I catch you, this shit is over with," I replied.

"Yea, yea, yea... Just keep playing with your computer and stop sending threats. Do you not realize I have been a step ahead of you each time? You can't win!" Julie stated.

"If you're a step ahead, why are you calling my phone and sending me threats. Why aren't you long gone, after what transpired yesterday? You're gonna have every cop in the city on your ass in a moment."

"Empty ass threats," she replied.

"Where is it, Julie?" I asked her, suspicious of a camera in the room.

"Sorry, Richard, I gotta go," Julie hurried. "Oh yeah, don't tell Jamie we've spoken. We don't need to scare her any more than she already is."

Julie hung up and Jamie came out of the washroom in her robe.

"Your aunt; there's a camera somewhere in this room and she is watching us," I spoke as I pointed to my phone.

"Now what?" Jamie questioned as she dried her hair with the towel.

"All we can do is wait, Jamie. As soon as you're ready, we will leave so we can get the day started." I responded.

Soon, Jamie was ready, and we left the room carrying all of the bags.

We waited at the front desk for the car. Valet parking pulled the car around the front and the driver exited the vehicle.

"Michael!" Jamie spoke excitedly, running over to hug him.

"How's my favorite baby cousin?" Michael asked.

"I'm fine. Ricky, this is my cousin, Michael."

Jamie was unaware that I already knew Michael.

"How have you been Michael?" I asked him, surprised at his unexpected arrival.

"Things have been pretty well, Richard," Michael spoke. "Just keeping myself busy. I work here, now," he answered. "And when they radioed for ticket 64 and I saw the name, I had to be the one to bring it to you," he finished.

"I'm glad to see that things are going well for you," I replied as I continued to look around.

"You seem like you're in a rush," he replied.

"Your cousin. She's up to her old antics," I shook my head. "We've gotta get out of here."

"You all know each other?" Jamie asked.

I cleared my throat.

"Yes baby," I spoke.

"Detective Young cleared me of the bank robbery charges that your aunt was involved in, Jamie," Michael finished as he gave me a look.

Jamie put her hand over her mouth.

"I didn't realize she's been doing this for so long," Jamie slightly shook her head.

"It's been a while," I replied. "Look, Michael, I'm sorry to cut this short, but we've gotta get moving if we want to stay from Julie's crosshairs."

"You're right. I'll try to talk to her," Michael said. "I will catch up with y'all later," he finished.

I got in the driver's seat and Jamie got in the passenger seat.

"How long are you working today, Michael?" Jamie asked through the window.

"I'm here until about 5 today, baby girl," he answered.

"Okay. I'll catch up with you then. I love you," Jamie responded.

"I love you, too," Michael stated.

Michael walked inside of the hotel and I drove off.

"Ricky," Jamie spoke a few seconds after I merged onto the expressway. "I want to move in with you for safety and because I feel like I'm in heaven when I'm with you. My aunt knows where I live and could try anything," she finished.

"That sounds good to me," I started. "Let's go to my old home first; the insurance guy is going to meet me there, find somewhere new that I can immediately move into, and we'll go from there, baby," I finished.

"I love you, Ricky," she stated.

"I love you too, Jamie."

12

Months passed and I'd purchased and moved into my new home. Jamie and I were living together, and surprisingly, we hadn't heard a word from Julie. She'd been silent ever since we left the *Plaza Galleria*.

Jamie was sitting on the bed when my phone rang.

"Hello," Jamie answered.

"No need for words. Just listen. Stay away from my man, okay?" the voice replied.

"Um," Jamie started as she looked at the phone, "I believe you have the wrong number."

"Is this Richard's phone? Detective Young?"

Jamie was stunned at this information.

"It is, but what does that —," she continued.

"Which must make you his damsel in distress," the voice interrupted. "Look, just stay away from my man. You were merely a distraction so that we could start our life together."

"Excuse you?" Jamie asked.

The person didn't reply but hung up and a picture message came through.

Jamie looked at the image of me and the woman.

"Wow, I can't believe this shit," she replied.

She put the phone down and took off the necklace I gave her, as well as the ring.

"Jamie... I need your opinion, baby—" I started and noticed the tears in her eyes. "What's wrong, baby?" I asked her.

"Ricky, do you remember what you told me about the necklace?" she asked as she held the tears back from falling.

"Yes, Jamie. The inside is our love and outside are the temptations that try to separate us." I told her, still confused as to why she was asking this.

"And the ring represents eternity," Jamie whispered.

"Baby, what's wrong?"

"All this time!" she yelled, throwing my phone and her ring at me.

I ducked at the precise moment and the phone missed me. Jamie walked towards me and slapped me. She left out of the room and walked towards the next room across the hall.

Confused, I followed her out of the room.

"Jamie, what is all of this about?" I asked.

Jamie didn't hold back any longer and exploded.

"Who is this bitch you were with last night when you were supposed to be working?" Jamie asked as she raised her tone.

"Babe, I *was* working last night," I emphasized.

"Don't give me that bullshit. I saw the pictures and your bitch just called," Jamie opened the dresser and got some clothes out. "You know what the fuck I've been through, yet you want to put me through it again," she finished.

I decided I wasn't going to do anything to provoke her anger. "Baby, tell me what is going on," I stated calmly.

She ignored me as she closed the dresser. She brushed against me as she passed me.

I grabbed her arm and pulled her back to me.

I pinned her against the wall.

"I need for you to speak to me and tell me what is going on," I demanded.

I could see the hurt in Jamie's eyes, but I couldn't decipher if she was more-so hurt, angry, or afraid at this moment.

Her lip quivered as she replied to me.

"Richard, let me go!" she demanded.

I decided to let her go, seeing as though when she got like this, it was best to just let her calm down.

She slapped me with the necklace in her hand; she dropped the necklace to the floor.

She brushed past me again and walked to the house phone.

"Hey, Aunt Julie," Jamie started to speak.

I walked to the washroom sink and began to clean the cut that the necklace had left behind. I looked in the mirror, confused as to what just happened.

As I heard her say Julie's name, anger entered my body.

"Auntie, I need for you to come to pick me up; things have gone left with Richard. I think he was just using me," she announced over the phone. "I know, I know. Yes, I'm getting ready now. Thank you, Auntie. See you in ten minutes. I love you." Jamie hung up and looked up, only to see me in the doorway.

"So that's it? You're just gonna walk out on me? And I have no idea as to why you're leaving? Because some female sent you a few pictures?" I asked her.

"My aunt will be here in a moment, Ricky. I must go." Jamie placed the necklace in my hand and lugged two suitcases downstairs. "I'll be back for the rest of my stuff later," Jamie stated.

I opened the door to my home and stood there with Jamie as she awaited Julie's arrival.

"So, this is it?" I asked again.

"Richard, it's for the best that we just dropped this," she spoke. "This relationship was a façade from the very start. I was merely a witness to help you try to catch my aunt. You haven't been able to do so, so there's no further need for me," she finished.

"Jamie, you know I love you," I retaliated.

Jamie wiped her eyes with her hand.

"And I love you, too," she sniffled. "But I'm going to love you from afar," she kissed me on the cheek.

Julie pulled up in a black, metallic-colored car.

Directly behind her were 3 more cars; exact replicas to the first. They all had the same design, license plate number, same everything; each car filled with men dressed in black.

Julie slowly approached my porch while being followed by the men, who all seemed to exit their vehicles in unison.

"Jamie, here. I want you to keep this," I told her, putting the necklace around her neck.

When I finished securing the necklace, she kissed me on the cheek again and walked off of the porch.

Two of the men grabbed Jamie's bags and walked them over to the car.

"Richard, I told you that I'm always ahead of you, whether you want to believe it or not," Julie studied me up and down. "It seems to me like you didn't use your better sense in judgment with dating this time around. Congratulations, you just flirted with death," Julie smirked.

"Julie, I should arrest you right now," I stated.

"If you really wanna try that right now, go on," she tested my intelligence, seeing as though it was one of me and sixteen of them. "Exactly! You're a smart guy. Just made a dumbass decision," Julie stated when I just stood back. "Boys," she stated while walking off.

The men all started to walk towards me.

"You ready for this ass whooping?" one of the men asked.

"Not without a fair fight," said a voice coming from behind the crowd. "15 of y'all and one of him? That just doesn't seem fair," the person came to the front and walked on the porch.

I was surprised to see Jared. He held out his badge and flashed his gun.

"Now, why don't y'all waive on out of here and we will just let this slide?" Jared stated to the men.

"We can't do that, we have a job to complete," one of the men spoke. She left specific orders," he finished.

"Well, it's not going to be a 15 to one fight. You mess with Richard, you mess with me," Jared stated.

"Alright. We're prepared to deal with that," the man stated.

I looked at Jared to see if he was serious. He looked at me and mouthed out the question, 'you ready?'.

I nodded my head in reply.

One of the men walked towards me and I kicked him. I shoved the man to the ground and attacked the next man that came for me. Another guy went for Jared.

Jared and I continued to fight the men until only one man was standing.

Upon seeing he was the last man standing and the rest were injured on the ground, he grabbed Jared and pulled out his gun.

I pulled out mine and aimed it at the man.

"Drop your gun!" I demanded.

"Rich, aim low," Jared instructed.

"Jared, he has a gun to your head; and you want him to live?" I asked.

"Dead suspects can't tell us shit," Jared replied.

"Well, neither do live ones," I chuckled.

I could tell Jared was trying to keep conversation to distract the man long enough to find a way out of it.

"Listen to your boy; you better aim low. You don't want to be fired, do you?" the suspect interrogated.

"Is that what you think will happen?" I asked. "I'll splatter your shit over this lawn."

"You want me to do his ass?" the man asked.

"Do me? What the fuck?" Jared asked. "Nah, bruh, I'm good."

"A little suspect if you ask me," I replied to the man as he readjusted the gun.

"I think you're smarter than you think," he snickered.

"Oh, so you're thinking that because you have a gun to my boy's head, I won't put one in you," I threatened. "I'll do it and no fucks would be given."

"Is that right?" Jared asked.

"That's right," I spoke. "You ready to die, bro?" I asked him.

"The fuck?" Jared asked. "Why would I want to do that?"

"Stop all the damn talking," the man demanded.

I shot at the sprinkler on the lawn beside him. The sprinkler turned on, causing water to spray on the man and confused him for a second, giving Jared the chance to turn around and punch the man.

Jared got the man on the ground and put his knee is the man's back.

I rose to my feet and aimed my gun at the remaining men on the ground.

"All of you all, turn over on your stomachs and put your hands behind your backs," I said. "Cross your feet."

The men groaned in pain but managed to turn over on their stomachs. They followed my direction as I aimed the gun at them.

"We need several cars here at Detective Richard Young's house," Jared stated over his radio.

"You all will be going to jail today. You will be booked, processed, and jailed," I told the men.

The men were silent. I could tell they we disappointed that things didn't go the way they'd planned.

"Rick, why are they here anyway?" Jared questioned as he secured his handcuffs on the final man that he'd fought.

"Jamie left and Julie picked her up," I slightly shook my head. "She brought 'security' with her," I added. "Seems to me like they failed at the one job they had," I laughed.

Jared chuckled and walked over to me.

"Let's go on and pat these gentlemen down as we wait for the others," I directed.

"Do you all have anything on you that may poke or injure us?" Jared asked.

"Firearms in the vehicles, but not on us," one of the men spoke, still face down.

Jared and I started to frisk the men; Jared started from the man on the far-left side and I started on the right side. The plan was to meet in the middle.

"Why didn't you want me to shoot his ass?" I asked Jared. while frisking the men.

"Because we wouldn't have anything but a dead suspect. When he's alive, he can be tried, and we can get some answers," Jared answered.

"So, if he'd pulled the trigger, you would be dead, and he would have a hole in his leg," I chuckled.

"But he didn't shoot though," Jared added.

"That's beside the point. I just want to know that if someone has a gun aimed at me and was a threat to my life, I wanna know that you gonna smoke his ass," I told him. "Fuck that therapy, 'let's talk it out', aim low shit. Real-life though," I told Jared.

"I got you, bro," Jared laughed. "Command received."

I chuckled as we stood side by side with our guns aimed at the men in case they tried to do anything.

Moments later, we heard several police vehicles coming down the street.

The police got out of their vehicles and put the men in handcuffs. For the men who didn't have steel handcuffs, the officers used the heavy-duty zip-tie handcuffs to restrain the suspects. They confiscated the weapons the men had and put them in the back seat of the cars.

"What happened here?" an officer asked Jared and me.

"We had to fight," I chuckled. "Book them all on assault on police officers and trespassing," I finished as I ensured my weapon was secure in the holster.

The police finished putting the men in the back of their vehicles and drove away.

"So now what, Rick?" Jared asked me.

"You're my bro, Jared. No matter what may have happened in the past," I replied.

"Aw man, don't even trip. You know I got your back." Jared responded.

"I can't let you know that enough," I reiterated.

"Man, I said don't sweat it," he laughed, "I got you."

I clapped Jared's hand and followed with a quick embrace.

"Let's head down there and make sure these bastards are processed," Jared spoke.

"Let's go."

***

Upon entering the police station, Jared walked towards Abel's office and I walked into mine. I closed the door behind myself and sat down, putting my hands on my head. When I looked up, I saw Linda standing there. I immediately rose to my feet.

"What are you doing here Linda?" I asked her.

"Just checking up on you, and to make sure you leave Julie alone," she stated.

"You and Julie don't have to worry about me for a long time; that is, considering you leave my office right now," I inched towards the door.

"No, I can't do that, how do I know if I can trust you?"

"You can if you leave," I told her.

Linda walked back towards the door.

"It's too late," she stated, turning around. "If I leave now, it will be ruined."

"Linda, what are you talking about?" I asked her.

"This is what I'm talking about," she stated as she pulled out a gun and aimed it at me.

I quickly tried to reach for my gun.

"Don't try that, Richard!" Linda demanded.

"Linda," I stated calmly. "You are in a police station and," I noticed the gun she had, "there are at least 120 officers and 20 SWAT team members here right now. You only have about 10-12 bullets in that gun; you won't survive."

"Do you really think I came in here unprepared?" she asked with a smirk.

Jared walked into the office. As soon as he saw Linda's gun aimed at me, he pulled out his.

"Richard, what the hell is she doing here?" Jared asked.

"The hell if I know," I spoke. "Ask her."

Linda quickly aimed her gun at Jared, giving me just enough time to grab my gun.

I aimed my gun at Linda.

"Put the gun down, Linda," I stated.

She looked and noticed the two guns aimed at her.

In an instant, she pushed me down to the floor. My gun flew from my hand as I fell, and she kicked the gun away from my reach. Linda continued to aim at Jared.

Jared firmly held his gun.

"You good, bro?" he asked me while I was on the ground.

I didn't want to provoke Linda, so I avoided moving.

"I'm good," I told him.

Linda aimed her gun at me and I drew my ankle gun.

I shot her once in her leg and watched her fall.

Other officers heard the gunshot and rushed into my office with their guns prepared.

Abel made his way to the front of the crowd.

"What's going on here?" Abel asked.

He lowered his weapon as he saw me on the ground. He looked to his right and saw Linda.

I rose to my feet.

"Threat to the force," I explained as I put my weapon away. I picked up my other gun as well.

Officers lifted Linda to her feet and I glared at her.

"Linda tried to kill Jared and me. She even indirectly threatened the force," I added.

I could tell that Abel was disgusted at what occurred.

"Get this piece of shit out of my sight," Abel spoke.

"I'm going to need for you all to be gentle," she spoke. "I didn't even do shit!"

I patted Abel on the back and walked over to my seat. I slumped down in the chair.

"You okay, man?" Jared asked.

"Hell no," I replied.

What happened with Jamie was finally settling in, and it had my head in circles. And with Linda coming in pulling this stunt, it drove me over the edge.

"I'm done," I started. "I can't continue to chase behind these two. Linda and Julie won't have to worry about me anymore. I'm turning this case over." I mentioned.

"Meaning?" Jared questioned.

I didn't answer him. I rose from the chair and walked out of the room.

13

Many months passed and I hadn't attempted to contact Julie, Linda, or Jamie.

Jared and I solved many more cases and were bringing slight shame to the other officers in the unit.

"Rick, bring your slow ass on," Jared joked from the front of the police station, eager to go home.

"Blah!" I shouted in reply.

I closed my office door and ensured it was locked before walking to the front of the station.

"You ready to go?" I asked him with a chuckle.

"Goodbye," he laughed and left out of the station.

We both entered our vehicles, and both drove in the direction of Jared's home.

Once we arrived, Madison was at the door with 3-month old Jacob, their newborn son.

"Baby!" Jared spoke excitedly as he exited the car and walked up to her.

He kissed her passionately.

"Y'all need to chill all that," I laughed. "That's how Jacob was made," I explained while exiting my vehicle.

"Ricky!" Madison shouted excitedly.

She handed Jacob to Jared and walked over to me.
She embraced me.

"Hey Madison," I replied, accepting her embrace. "How have you been?" I asked as we both retreated.

"I've been good; tired and busy with Jacob, but good. How about yourself?" Madison asked as I walked toward the house.

"Busy with the job and all. Haven't really had much time for anything," I chuckled.

"That sucks," she stated. "No freedom at all?" she reiterated.

"I wouldn't say no freedom," I started, "but not too much fun. Besides kicking ass alongside your husband," I laughed.

Jared laughed at my joke.

"But you have time to eat, right, bro?" Jared questioned.

"Yea, I guess so," I gave in. "I can always go for food," I chuckled.

"Your fat ass," Jared joked.

Madison laughed and we all walked inside.

Jared walked to the table and sat down and Madison brought his food to him.

"Baby, let Richard hold Jacob," Jared stated to Madison as he unrolled his silverware.

I felt a slight hint of nervousness pass through my body after the words left Jared's mouth.

"It's okay, Madison, I don't want to be..." I started.

"Bro, stop acting like that and take your nephew," Jared stated with a chuckle.

Madison passed me the small infant and stepped back. I looked at the infant as he gurgled and played with my index finger.

"He likes you, Rick," Jared stated.

"I guess so," I stated.

I immediately felt a connection to him; I probably even developed a small ounce of baby fever as I held and played with him.

"You know, babies have a way of distinguishing good from bad. All it takes is one hold, and they can tell who's good and who isn't," Madison spoke.

"I guess he's saying that I'm one of the good guys," I replied.

***

"Rick, you need to hurry back. You quickly take to your nephew. Don't leave my baby boy, heartbroken," Jared chuckled.

"Bring him to the station sometime," I joked.

"Yeah, right," Jared scoffed.

I laughed in reply.

"Hurry back Richard," Madison stated. "We love you."

"I will. I love y'all too," I stated and got into my car.

Jared put his arm around Madison and waved a hand at me. I flashed my bright lights on the car and I drove off. I didn't turn on any music, news, or anything. All that could be heard was the sound of the engine and car accelerating.

***

I arrived home and walked into my room. I walked to the bed and fell forward onto it.

I laid on the bed and I turned my head to the right.

I saw a picture of Jamie and myself.

A phone call abruptly interrupted my thoughts.

"Hello," I stated answering the call without looking at the caller ID.

"Hello? Ricky?" the voice whispered.

"Who is this?" I asked.

"Aunt Julie's going to kill me," Jamie let out a quiet cry.

Hearing Jamie's voice was something I needed, but not to hear her in this state. It worried me deeply to hear that she was in trouble.

"Baby, don't worry. I will not let that happen. Where are you?" I asked sitting up in the bed.

"I'm not sure. I just know we left Oklahoma not too long ago and we're entering Texas. She had to stop for gas and left me in the car," I could hear Jamie was panicking. "It's a blue Dodge Charger, license plates H23-FWD," Jamie stated. "Ricky, she's coming," Jamie whispered in a hurry.

"Baby, I'm going to find out where you are," I assured her as I secured my holster to my belt. "Please, leave your phone on. I will be there soon." I told her while I was walking down the stairs.

"I love you, Ricky," she stated and quickly hung up.

"I love you too, Jamie," I stated, even though I knew she had hung up.

I locked the door to my home and ran towards my car. I started it and raced to the police station.

I hurried inside of the building and rushed into my office.

Other officers saw me in a hurry and followed me into my office.

"Young, what's going on?" an officer asked.

I didn't reply to him.

I picked up my phone to call Jamie, but I didn't get an answer. Instead, I received a text from her stating that she couldn't answer because her aunt was in the car.

"Come on, baby," I spoke aloud as I texted her back, asking her to answer so that I could get a signal.

I redialed her number and placed the phone on the tracker.

The tracker quickly picked up her location, based on the towers that her phone was receiving pings from.

I composed an email on my work computer and sent it to Double X-L and multiple news outlets.

Subject: Abduction
Priority: High
Hey everyone,
This is Detective Richard Young of the Chicago Police Department, and I need you all to air this abduction alert. It is for Jamie Perez: she's of Puerto Rican descent, light skin, medium length hair, brown eyes, about 5'2", 115-120 pounds, small birthmark on left shoulder. She was last seen with her aunt, Julie Wilson; blue Dodge Charger, Illinois license plate, H23-FWD. They were last seen crossing the Texas border from Oklahoma. Suspect is armed and dangerous. If you happen to see Jamie Perez, Julie

Wilson, or the vehicle they may be traveling in, contact the
authorities! Let's bring Jamie home, safely.
Thanks in advance, everyone!

I sent the email and locked my machine.

I watched the television inside of the station. A few moments later, the notice came on the television, with the image of Jamie I'd attached.

As the alert went off, my phone rang.

"Rick, what the fuck is going on? What is this about Jamie being missing with Julie?" he asked.

"Bro, I can't explain now. Kiss Madison and Jacob and meet me at my house in twenty minutes. We're gonna take us a little trip."

I knew Jared could hear the anger and fear in my voice.

"I got you, bro. Don't sweat it, we're going to get her back," he spoke before hanging up.

The officers in the office all swarmed around me as the alert went off.

"Guys, I don't have a game plan, just yet. I'll give you all a call once I get home and figure this out," I announced.

"You should have told us sooner," an officer spoke.

I shook my head.

"I'll update you all with what happens," I spoke as I walked away. "Make sure you all suit up and are ready," I projected as I left the building.

I sped home and found Jared leaning again my garage, using his phone.

"What's the word?" Jared asked as I got out of my vehicle.

"Jamie is on her own with Julie," I spoke, disgustedly. "Julie is going to kill her. We gotta go get her," I spoke as I pressed in my code to my garage door.

The door opened and I walked over to the box that resided on the side table.

"Shit, but we only have a little bit of time to do it, so we're going by air," I tossed Jared my keys.

"Fuck," Jared spoke. "We should have known that things would escalate to this with Julie. All of her crimes that she's committed have been getting more and more clever."

"Yeah, but not smarter than us," I spoke.

I pulled ammunition from the box and put it to the side. I also pulled out two armored vests and a few of the pistols and small automatic weapons that I possessed.

I loaded the items into my car and closed the garage door. As the door was closing, Jamie called me.

"Talk to me, baby," I answered.

"Ricky, my aunt heard your announcement. She is becoming suspicious because it was on every station here, including digital billboards. She knows that I'm in contact with you," Jamie whispered.

I hadn't taken a moment to think about Julie figuring out that Jamie was in contact with me, but I decided to look at the positive outcome.

"Good, maybe she will stop," I stated. "She knows I'm involved, and she knows that I'll stop at nothing to keep you safe."

"No Ricky, it's not good," Jamie explained. "She's switching cars. I'm over here by the Charger and she's getting a new one. A lime green Hummer. License plate 872-3-," Jamie spoke.

"What the fuck?!" Julie shouted as she came to the phone. "Who is this?" she asked as she took the phone from Jamie.

I remained silent.

"Richard?" Julie questioned; I could tell she had a grin on her face.

Again, I didn't reply.

"I know it's you. Your witness has you saved in her phone," Julie spoke.

I heard Jamie groan.

"You're hurting me," Jamie spoke to Julie.

I finally decided to speak.

"Julie, if you do anything to Jamie," I started, "you will have a shit-storm on you," I threatened.

"Oh, threats," Julie cackled.

I could hear her strike Jamie.

Julie laughed as Jamie made a noise in pain. She then hung up the phone.

"Son of a bitch!" I shouted and slammed the garage door shut.

Jared walked over and put his hand on my shoulder.

"Fucking Julie, man," I spoke in disgust.

"It'll be okay, bro," Jared tried to comfort me. "We just gotta keep our heads."

I didn't reply to Jared. Instead, I pulled out my phone to call Abel.

"I heard the announcement," Abel answered. "I'm gearing up now," he added. "What's the plan?"

It was good to know how he was on top of it.

"I am going to drive to the airport and get the chopper and you all will just have to trail behind me," I spoke as Jared and I got into the car. I continued speaking, "all choppers have GPS chips in them, so pinpoint my location and move out."

"I'm on my way to the airport now. I'll radio the other officers."

Abel hung up the phone and I closed the car door.

I put my head on the steering wheel.

"Bro, we will save her. Don't even worry," Jared assured me.

"I hope you're right," I told him.

I drove to the airport as quickly as possible and Jared unloaded the items from the car and transferred them into the helicopter, as I started the aircraft. As we finished loading everything, I locked the car and we both climbed into the helicopter.

I turned on my laptop and it picked up the reception to Jamie's phone. Audio and video transmitted over my laptop from Jamie's jacket.

"Seems like we're stranded, Jamie," Julie spoke. "I'll hold on to this," she spoke as she showed Jamie the phone.

The screen appeared to be off, but I knew the phone couldn't have been if I was able to sustain a connection.

"We will stay here overnight and then we're going to cross the border. Then it's time to go night-night. I should have done this a long time ago; you fuckin' snake!" Julie hissed at Jamie.

"Location from the phone is showing Albuquerque, New Mexico. We have to hurry," I stated over my radio.

I continued to fly the helicopter as the rain began to fall from the clouds.

***

Hours passed and we were in New Mexico, approaching the Mexico border.

"The GPS to the phone says we're right above them," I spoke to Jared.

Jared looked through the camera and didn't see anything.

"There's no one below us," he spoke.

"Roberts, let's lower these birds," I spoke. "The phone's GPS location is showing that we are right above them, but I'm not seeing anything on the camera."

"10-4," Abel spoke moments later. "Dropping the helicopters."

We both lowered the helicopters completely and looked around as we got out.

"There's nothing here," I shook my head and displayed a look of confusion on my face.

"Julie thinks she's a damn genius," Jared spoke as he came around to where I stood.

Abel also approached me.

"Thoughts?" I asked.

"There's no way she's going to let us catch her this easily," Jared spoke. "Remember the bank robbery?"

"Shit, you're right," I replied as I walked back to my computer, which resided in the helicopter.

"There's nothing here," Abel spoke over the radio. "Isabella, do we have any hits on the alert?"

"None yet," Isabella spoke. "Well, nothing that's legitimate."

"Fuck, fuck, fuck," I shouted as I viewed the screen.

"What's wrong, Richard?" Abel asked.

"Motherfucker's been playing us," I spoke as I brought the computer from the helicopter and showed them the screen. "The jacket is showing a location right in between El Paso, Texas and Ciudad Juarez in Chihuahua."

"Mexico?" Abel asked aloud. "They aren't going to let us in easily."

"Well, let's hope she's in El Paso, Texas," Jared replied. "Get these birds back in the sky," he shouted as Abel turned back towards his helicopter.

Jared ran over to the passenger side of the helicopter and climbed inside and I got into the pilot's seat. I was still able to get a connection to the microphone and video feed from the jacket, so I tuned into the feed. The camera displayed a dark screen.

"Jamie," I called over the channel to the earpiece.
I didn't get a reply.
"Fuck," I spoke aloud. "Roberts, I'm not getting an answer from the subject."
"We'll get there as soon as we can, Young," Abel assured me as we both flew our helicopters. "Keep the signal coming from the jacket."

"I think Julie is using random cell towers to bounce off for the phone, because she knew that we would use the location to find out where they are," Jared spoke over the radio.
"Well, she didn't know about the jacket. So let's beat her at her own game," I uttered.
***
All of the officers exited the helicopter that they sat in with their guns drawn.
"I don't get it," I spoke as I scratched my head. "The GPS is saying that we're standing in the exact location."

"Alright, everyone, keep looking around," Abel announced. "Our target is Jamie Perez; the suspect is Julie Wilson."
"This is the desert; look for any disturbed land," I feared for the worst as I paced the sand. Jared stood by my side and walked with me.

"I just can't imagine if I lose her," I admitted to Jared.
"We can't fear the worst," Jared replied. "We'll get her and soon, she'll back in your arms."
Jared put his arm around my shoulder and we continued to walk, and I squatted down.

"Gentlemen," Jared called to the other officers as I began to use my hand to sift through the sand.
"This land has been disturbed," I spoke.

I dug with my hands and the other officers squatted down to assist me.

I dug faster and my hand ran across what felt like a finger. "I got something!" I exclaimed.

My heart raced once I felt the finger. Jared dusted the sand from the hand, and I could tell from the bracelet that was on the wrist that it belonged to Jamie.

I struggled to fight the tears that accumulated in my eyes.

"Dig, dig, dig," I shouted to the other officers; I was soon able to see her face, and I couldn't help the tears from falling.

"Let's get her up," Jared spoke as he could see my emotions.

"We've found the subject," Abel spoke over his radio. He didn't give a status update on her condition.

We all pulled her from the sand and I laid her down. I saw blood emitting from her shirt. I slightly raised the piece of clothing and saw a gunshot wound on her side.

I quickly removed my jacket and held it over her wound.

I put my fingers on her neck and felt a faint pulse.

"I got a faint pulse," I spoke as I began CPR. "Call a bus," I pressed on Jamie's chest.

I think every officer there could identify with the pain I was feeling as I performed CPR on Jamie.

Abel called for an ambulance over the radio and I continued the chest compressions.

"Come on, baby," I spoke before pinching her nose and breathing into her mouth.

I could hear Jared say a small prayer.

"The ambulance is around the corner," Abel shouted.

"I'm gonna fucking kill Julie," I whispered as I continued to try to resuscitate Jamie. "Come on, baby. Breathe, damn it," I spoke.

The ambulances were arriving at the scene when Jamie coughed and started to breathe.

I quickly held her head up and hugged her, even though she was coughing. I was careful and mindful of her wound as I held her.

Jamie winced with pain as she coughed to catch her breath.

"Subject is alive, with a gunshot wound to her lower left abdomen," Abel finally reported over the radio as he took off his vest and walked over to me.

I couldn't stop kissing Jamie on the cheek as I held her tightly. The tears fell during this moment.

"Baby," she whispered.

"Don't say a word right now, baby," I told her as the paramedic unloaded from the ambulance.

"Suspect Julie Wilson is still on the run," Abel spoke over the radio once more as he kneeled to me.

"I thought I lost you," I shook my head as I silently wept to Jamie.

"Baby, I love you," Jamie whispered as she coughed.

"Shhh," I silenced her.

I could feel that Jamie loved me, and I knew that she could tell how much I loved her. It pained me to see her in this state; I was furious and determined to catch her aunt.

"Jared, make sure they get that bitch," I whispered to him as the paramedics unloaded from the ambulance.

He put Jamie on a stretcher and connected her to machines within the ambulance, and his partner proceeded to speak to us.

"Her vitals and everything are normal. We will be taking her to the hospital to treat her wound and ensure that everything is okay. Give me a rundown of what happened," he spoke to me in a gruff voice.

"You know that abduction alert that was put out?" Jared started. "Jamie Perez: found nearly unconscious buried under sand with a gunshot wound to the side."

The paramedic shook his head.

"Officer, we'll do everything we can. She seems like she's going to be okay, though," he added before walking back to the ambulance.

"Young," Abel called to me.

"Yes?" I questioned, never taking my eyes off of the ambulance.

"Go on with her to the hospital," he spoke in a calm tone. "We'll take everything from here," he patted my shoulder.

"You sure, Abel?" I questioned.

"Go on," he reiterated. "Let's get these birds in the air and find the suspect," he announced to the other officers.

I walked to the ambulance and got in the back of the vehicle. The paramedic closed the back door and walked around to the passenger side.

The ambulance drove off with the sirens on.

I sat on the side as the medical team monitored Jamie's vitals. I held her hand tightly.

"I'll never let you go, again," I spoke to Jamie as I kissed her hand. "I love you."

***

"We got her," Jared spoke over the phone. "Son of a bitch was leaving Texas, but she stopped for gas and was flagged by the ping of the nearby cell tower," Jared explained. "You already know that she's denying involvement."

"We'll worry about all of that later," I slightly shook my head. "Bro," I said, "thank you," I stared at Jamie, admiring her beauty more than ever.

I hung up the phone and walked over to the hospital bed that Jamie was laying in. I leaned down and kissed her on the forehead.

"Is that all you got for me?" she asked with a chuckle.

I smiled and kissed her on the lips.

"That's more like it," she smiled and held my hand.

I sat on the bed beside her.

"They got her," I told Jamie.

A look of relief crossed her face, but she didn't say anything.

"Baby, I know you may not be feeling the best right now," I spoke. "But I need for you to tell me everything that went down following my connection with you."

"I can't forget," Jamie remembered, "after I spoke to you on the phone, we went to a motel, where we spent the night. From there, she took me to the Texas-Mexico border, and ordered me to exit the car," Jamie spoke as a small tear fell down her eye.

"Take your time, baby," I wiped her tear.

Jamie continued.

"I fought back; I wasn't about to just get out of the car and end up stranded. On top of that, I hadn't even heard from you, so I didn't know what was going on," she admitted. "So then, during our struggle and her attempt to get me out of the car, the gun went off," she shuddered a little. "I don't think she meant for it to happen, but when I was hit, she panicked, and the last thing I remember was a pillow going over my face."

My heart felt for Jamie, and my anger for Julie grew.

"Do you know about what time this was, baby?" I asked her.

"Richard, I wouldn't know," Jamie admitted. "The time was the very last thing on my mind," she chuckled.

I put a hand on Jamie's face and couldn't help but scan her body. My eyes became fixated on her side where the gunshot wound was.

"You're safe now, baby," I spoke, followed by another kiss on the lips.

14

Two years passed since the hostage situation with Julie and Jamie, and the court date had arrived.

Julie was arrested following the situation, but naturally, she denied any involvement. She insisted that the whole event was created by Jamie and me to put her away; that was her story and she was sticking with it.

I sat at the foot of the bed as I watched Jamie adjust her hair in the mirror.

"Ricky, I don't feel so good about this," Jamie nervously admitted. "I just don't feel right testifying against my aunt."

I got off of the bed and walked towards her.

"Jamie," I started.

I stopped walking once I was face-to-face with her. I lifted the side of her shirt and made sure she saw where she was shot. "Remember what your aunt did to you; she wanted you to die. She shot you, suffocated you, and buried you, where you weren't found until at least two hours later," I spoke softly. "I will be right there the whole time," I assured Jamie and kissed her.

Jamie returned the kiss and hugged me tightly.

I could feel the fear in Jamie's body as we embraced, and I had to find a way to make sure she felt comfortable during this process.

"I've never gone against family," Jamie spoke. "Regardless of how many times they turned their back on me."

"I'm right here, Jamie," I whispered as I kissed her cheek.

I turned my head slightly and looked at the clock. It was almost time for the case.

"Come on, baby. It's about time to head out." I told her.

She could tell I was ready for the case and had been waiting for this day to come. I was dressed in an all-black suit, with my gun on my side with an extra magazine.

"You look like a million bucks," she joked.

"All the money in the world doesn't matter if I don't have you," I told her.

"Such a cake," she chuckled before walking down the stairs.

Jamie walked out of the house first and I followed her. We both got into my car and I drove to the airport to retrieve the helicopter.

I flew the helicopter to the landing pad near the courthouse and Jamie drove my car to the courthouse.

She waited for me to lock the helicopter and secure it to the pad, and we both entered the building.

The secretary directed us to the courtroom after we told her about the trial. Waiting outside of the courtroom was Jared, Abel, and a few other officers who seemed to not have a care in the world.

"You ready, Young?" Abel asked me.

"Are you kidding me?! This is the moment I've been waiting for," I spoke excitedly. "I'm ready to put Julie away and put an end to all of this madness," I answered. "However, Jamie is nervous about testifying against Julie."

"That's normal. It's her aunt. We have to make her as comfortable as possible during this trial," Abel replied.

A court officer stepped outside of the room.

"Can I have everyone's attention?" he spoke.

Everyone turned around and faced the officer.

"I am Deputy Thomas. The trial shall commence soon, but before it does, I need to do a routine check," he cleared his throat.

"Once we enter the courthouse, all cellphones are to be powered off. All beepers, pagers, and two-way radios should either be powered down or set to the lowest volume or vibrate. There are to be no loaded firearms in the courthouse, except for the Court Officer. Any law enforcement personnel are allowed to carry firearms and ammunition, but the safety mechanism must be enabled, and the weapon should not be loaded."

The deputy continued to speak, but I spaced out as I caught a glimpse of Julie being escorted to the courtroom. She saw me and made a face, but continued to walk with the officers.

"Do you all understand these rules as I have explained them to you?" Deputy Thomas asked.

"On behalf of the 24th District, all of the rules set forth shall and will be abided by while in the Court House," Abel spoke and shook the Deputy Thomas' hand.

Deputy Thomas opened the door and walked inside.

"You all may enter the room and take your seats. The Judge will be out shortly."

He took his position near the judge's desk and we all regrouped.

A few moments later, Michael entered the courtroom.

"How are you doing, Michael?" I asked as I shook his hand. "What brings you here, today?"

"I'm representing Julie Wilson," Michael replied.

"That's funny," I chuckled. "Stop joking around," I replied, "since when did you study law?"

Michael walked over to the Defense's stand and opened his briefcase.

"I guess there are plenty of things you don't know about me, Detective," he chuckled.

Deputy Thomas opened the door, and a police officer passed Julie to him. She was wearing a suit, and the smirk on her face told me that this was going to be a trial to remember.

Linda soon entered the courtroom and stood beside Michael.

"Sorry I'm late," she spoke to him as she hurried to put her bags down. "It's all good," Michael replied. "She's just now coming in," he added.

Deputy Thomas escorted Julie over to Michael, and he returned to where he previously stood.

"Looks to me like Linda is one of Julie's co-counsel in this trial," Jared spoke.

"Don't worry," I spoke with a satisfying smile as I looked at Linda. "We got something for that ass."

"Alright, squad, let's settle in and beat this case," Abel spoke to Jared, Jamie, and myself.

The rest of the officers took a seat in the audience row behind us.

The judge entered the room, and everyone rose to their feet.

"All rise! The honorable Judge Robert Stevens, presiding," Deputy Thomas spoke.

Once we were on our feet, six men similar to the ones that confronted Jared and me, entered the courtroom and sat behind the defense.

Deputy Thomas ordered the courtroom to sit, and the audience members took their seats.

"This is case number 4203, 'The People vs. Julie Wilson.'" Judge Stevens spoke. "Miss Wilson, you have previously entered a plea of 'not guilty'. Do you wish to change your plea?" he asked gruffly.

"No, Your Honor," Julie answered.

He sorted through a few papers, and put some in his drawer before looking up.

"Present your case," he stated.

"Your Honor, on August 21st, 2008, Julie Wilson was charged with robbery and money laundering, and was sentenced to seven years in prison. On September 3rd of 2011, Ms. Wilson was released from the Cook County Jail House, due to good behavior. About two weeks later, there was an incident at the Hancock building; leaving many officers injured and killed. Detective Young, myself, and Madeline Tucker surrounded and arrested the then-suspect, Jamie Perez," Jared started.

"Objection, Your Honor. If Jamie Perez was arrested and is a suspect, why would she be in the prosecutions' position?" Michael stated.

"Mr. Wilson, surely you must have learned from law school that there aren't any objections during opening statements. We save that for the actual testimony," the judge spoke. "I'm interested to hear where this goes," he added.

"Thank you, Your Honor. Upon arresting Ms. Perez, she was taken to the police station for questioning. It is here that she spoke with Detective Richard Young about her aunt, Julie Wilson, and how Ms. Wilson threatened her if she didn't proceed with the mission. Fearful for her life; she performed the action and tried to escape the police," Jared spoke while walking from behind the desk.

He paced the floor.

"Jamie proceeded to help the force, as it was issued instead of jail-time, to pursue her aunt. She would be an undercover unarmed officer. During this time, Julie Wilson instructed Jamie Perez of another case that she was to perform; we had Ms. Perez wired so we were able to see and hear everything that she was viewing and hearing. If we fast forward to the second mission, many were arrested, one suspect was killed, and a building was destroyed due to explosions set forth by the defendant, Julie Wilson," Jared removed his suit jacket and walked around to put it on his chair.

He paused briefly as he looked at the jurors.

"Ladies and gentlemen of the jury, the reason we are here today is because of an incident that occurred where the defendant kidnapped the victim, suffocated her, shot her, buried her, and left her for dead," his voice cracked. "Ever since Julie Wilson was released from prison, there has been situation after situation, crime after crime, and all things point back to her," Jared cleared his throat. "The CPD and Jamie Perez will adequately prove this, beyond a reasonable doubt, throughout this trial."

"We will now hear a statement from the defense," the judge stated.

Jared returned to the desk and shook hands with Madeline, Abel, and myself. Michael walked out to the center of the floor.

"Your Honor, I am here today to prove my client's innocence, and to show that this kidnapping case is no more than a misunderstanding; that Detective Young and the force are taking this to the extreme due to their dislike of my client. That is all," he stated with ease.

He looked in my direction and mouthed out 'game on' before returning to his seat.

"We will start with witnesses from the prosecution," the judge spoke.

"Your Honor, may I approach?" I asked.

"Permission granted."

I slowly walked to his desk and started to speak.

"Your Honor, we have a witness who isn't present. Is it possible to phone them?"

"Is this your first witness?" Judge Stevens asked.

"It is," I answered.

"Do you think they would be available to video-conference in for the set of questions? I'm certain they're prepared for this questioning, right?"

"I'm certain they can. With your permission, we'd like to give them a voice call and provide the information for them to call into the feed for questioning," I spoke.

"That's fine with me," the judge spoke to me. "This court is going to take a ten-minute recess," he announced to everyone. "Once we resume, we shall proceed with the first witness for the prosecution."

Judge Stevens banged his gavel and Deputy Thomas spoke.

"All rise!" he projected.

Everyone rose to their feet as the judge left the room and I returned to the desk.

During the recess, Jared called Madison and informed her that she would need to call into the courtroom via video-chat to answer questions. He provided her with the information and hung up.

Minutes later, the judge returned and settled the court.

"Are we all ready to go?" he asked.

"Yes, sir," I answered. "We would like to call Madison Hubbard as our first witness. We will be contacting her via Skype." I stated firmly.

"Bailiff," the judge stated firmly and the bailiff approached the desk to obtain her ID. The judge initiated a video call on the system and her video feed appeared on the screen.

"Hello?" Madison answered.

"Hello Madison, this is Judge Stevens from the Cook County courthouse. How are you doing this morning?"

"I'm good, how about yourself?"

"I'm very good. I know you may be busy, but if we could have a few minutes of your time, it will be greatly appreciated. There's a trial today, The City of Chicago vs. Julie Wilson and you have been called as a witness by the prosecution. Will you be willing to answer a few questions from both parties of this case?" he asked.

"Yes sir," Madison stated.

The deputy positioned himself in front of the camera holding a bible.

"Please raise your right hand," he spoke to Madison.

Madison raised her right hand before he continued.

"Do you swear to tell the truth, the whole truth, and nothing but the truth, so help you, God?"

"I do," Madison stated.

Abel walked over and positioned himself in front of the camera.

"Please state your full name, for the record," Abel spoke.

"Madison Veronica Hubbard."

"Miss Hubbard, do you know the defendant, Julie Wilson?" Abel asked her as he slightly motioned his body in Julie's direction.

"Yes, I know her," Madison spoke as she did a small eye roll.

"How do you know her?" Abel asked.

"Julie has attempted to kidnap me and kill me when I was pregnant," Madison spoke. "Linda Jackson, I only know that she is an accomplice to Julie Wilson and that she used to be a part of the Chicago police department," Madison finished.

"Objection; Linda Jackson was not mentioned in the question," Michael blurted.

"Sustained; the jury will disregard the statement about Linda Jackson," Judge Stevens announced.

"Mrs. Hubbard, do you know of the abduction alert that was issued on August 31st, 2012 for Jamie Perez?"

"I heard it on the news. It was withdrawn on the 1st of September if I recall correctly because you all had found her."

"Do you remember the details of the alert?" he asked inquisitively.

Madison thought for a moment.

"It was something about Julie Wilson having kidnapped Jamie Perez, and they were on the move from state-to-state. I think they were spotted in Oklahoma, or something like that," Madison said.

"Thank you, Miss Hubbard. No further questions, Your Honor," he finished.

Abel walked back to the desk and Michael stood in front of the camera.

"Good morning, Mrs. Hubbard," Michael introduced. "You say that my client has attempted murder, battery, and kidnapping. But, Chicago PD has listed her as a mastermind. The way they put it, if she wants to make something happen, she will. So, why is it that you accuse her of these things but none of them occurred?" Michael asked.

Madison thought before answering the question.

"Maybe she considered, but something foiled and altered her plans," Madison explained.

"Miss Hubbard, how do you know Detective Richard Young?" Michael asked as he decided to switch subjects.

"Objection. Relevance?" Abel projected.

"Overruled," Judge Stevens spoke.

"He's my ex, I met him shortly after an explosion at the Wilson residence, some years back."

"And is Hubbard your maiden name?" Michael asked with a smirk.

Madison emitted a small sigh.

"No, my maiden name is Miller."

"Oh, okay," Michael chuckled. "And who is it that changed your maiden name?"

"What the fuck?" Jared heard me mumble.

"I married Jared Hubbard," Madison stated.

"Jared Hubbard?" Michael asked. "You mean Jared Hubbard from the CPD?" he motioned in Jared's direction.

Madison sighed once more but didn't answer.

I put my hands on my head and Jared placed his hand on my shoulder.

"No further questions." Michael returned to his seat, feeling accomplished and arrogant.

"Thank you, Miss Hubbard, for allowing us a few minutes of your time," The judge ended the video call.

Judge Stevens cleared his throat with a sip of water before continuing.

"Defense's witness?"

"I would like to call Jared Hubbard to the stand," Michael replied with confidence.

Murmurs were scattered across from the jury and the audience.

Jared approached the stand, took the oath, and sat down.

"A lovely wife you have there," Michael stated.

"She's wonderful," Jared stated with attitude, in response to what Michael was doing.

I stepped out of the courtroom as Jared began speaking and I was followed by Abel.

"Is everything okay, Richard?" he asked me as he put his hands on my tie and adjusted it the way a father would do to his son.

"I'm just trying to think," I replied. "Michael's objective is to get this case dismissed so he's slowly pulling in bits and pieces from our personal lives. I'm trying to figure out a way to answer questions, without subjecting myself or this unit to failure." I told him.

"This is one reason I've always told you to leave personal issues at home," he answered. "But we're here now, and you know the force stands together no matter what," Abel added.

"You're absolutely right," I responded as I looked at the time.

A few moments of silence passed before Abel spoke again.

"We should probably get back inside. Simply to see how the questioning is going. Plus, we can't pass up the opportunity for a rebuttal with Jared," Abel spoke.

He entered the room and I followed directly behind him.

"So, is it safe to say that you have not had any personal interaction with my client?" Michael asked Jared. "And that all interactions have been in coordination with Detective Young?"

"No, it wouldn't be," Jared started. "Your client and I have had multiple interactions. The one I remember most is when she kidnapped my wife. For those few moments, I thought that I was going to lose her," Jared stated with his voice slightly cracking.

"No further questions, Your Honor." Michael took his seat and whispered something to Julie.

Since Madeline was present during Michael's line of questioning, we sent her up to present the set of rebuttal questions.

"Officer Hubbard, on the night in question, referring to the kidnapping and attempted murder of your wife; what were you doing at this time?" she asked Jared.

"I was instructed to report to Detective Young's home, due to a case of arson. I took Madison with me because I wasn't going to leave a pregnant woman alone."

"And what were you doing at the exact time your, now-wife then-girlfriend, was kidnapped?" she questioned.

"During the time Madison was kidnapped, I believe I may have been discussing a few pieces of information with Detective Young," Jared replied.

"Thank you," Madeline then looked at the judge. "No further questions, Your Honor," Madeline stated and returned to her seat.

Michael rose to his feet with a notepad.

"Officer Hubbard, really quickly, it is also reported that you and Detective Young had gotten into a physical altercation on that same night." Michael retorted. "Why is that?"

"Objection," Madeline stated. "Relevance?"

"Overruled," the judge stated. "Officer Hubbard, please answer the question."

"Is this judge working with the defense?" I whispered to Abel. "He is overruling all of our objections."

Abel tapped me on the shoulder to tell me to settle down.

"Detective Young and I did engage in an altercation; I can't remember the reason for it at the moment," Jared stated, not wanting to mention the fact we fought because of Madison.

"So, you remember what you were doing exactly at the time your girlfriend was kidnapped, but you can't remember why you and a fellow officer fought?" Michael asked as he raised an eyebrow.

"I said I don't know and that's the end of it," Jared stated, raising his tone slightly.

"No more questions, Your Honor."

Jared stepped down and Abel called Madeline to the stand.

After a series of questions and witnesses, the judge ordered the court to go to lunch.

All of the officers waited behind inside of the courtroom as the rest of the courtroom dispersed.

"What's on your mind, bro?" Jared asked me. He noticed I was the only officer sitting by myself.

"Michael's objective is to flip this case around; you notice the kinds of questions he's asking, right?" I asked.

"It's our job to not allow that to happen," Jared retorted.

"You're right," I spoke. "It's just funny as I think about the games he's playing," I said as I clicked my pen.

One of the men who sat behind Julie walked towards us.

"Look, not today. Just back up and go back to lunch," Jared spoke to him.

The guy raised his shirt and flashed an explosive, as well as an assault rifle. "Let's just be sure that Julie wins this case, cool?" he gruffly suggested. "Or else, these bullets in the assault rifle go towards your wife and child. You shouldn't have left them alone," he smirked.

He didn't give Jared a chance to respond; he walked out of the room.

"How in the hell does he get through the metal detectors with an assault rifle?" Jared questioned.

"I wonder who the fuck Julie really has on her payroll," I uttered as I shook my head. "We got some people doing some off-the-wall shit."

"This shit is crazy," Jared replied. "I'm about to go get his ass, fuck all that. And he threatened my wife and Jacob. It's on like Donkey Kong," Jared stuck out his chest and was about to walk in the direction of the man.

"Don't do it," I spoke as I extended my arm to stop him from walking. "Just go call Madison and tell her to get her and Jacob out of the home. I'll go let Abel know what just happened," I answered.

"Aight, cool," Jared replied. "And after this is all over and we're back to our civilian status, how about we go 'south side of Chicago' on that ass and fuck him up?" Jared chuckled.

"No doubt," I did my signature handshake with Jared before he stepped out of the courtroom to call Madison.

As Jared spoke to Madison, I approached Abel and the other officers to inform them of what just transpired.

Following lunch, the judge returned to the courtroom and Michael called his next witness.

"Your Honor, we would like to call Jamie Perez to the stand," Michael stated firmly.

I felt a chill run down my body.

As Jamie walked to the stand, so did Julie.

"Your Honor, with the court's permission, I would like to have my client Julie Wilson perform these series of questions."

"Permission granted." the judge stated.

"How, Sway?!" I asked aloud.

Judge Stevens looked at me sternly.

Abel shrugged his shoulders and tapped me on mine.

"Jamie Perez," Julie started with a smirk. "How old are you, sweetie?"

"I'm 28," Jamie replied, slightly scared and nervous.

Occasionally, she would look over to me for comfort, and Julie noticed this.

"And what do you do for a living?"

"I'm a student," Jamie answered.

"Now, it was stated that you were also an undercover police officer," Julie reminded the court.

"Part-time. My primary focus, at the moment, is my life and my schooling," Jamie added gracefully.

"Part-time?" Julie asked. "Can you produce any check stubs for this position if necessary?"

"Objection, Your Honor. How does this information correlate with the case?" Jared asked.

"Ms. Wilson, get to the point," Judge Stevens spoke.

Julie slightly nodded her head.

"Right," she spoke softly. She directed her attention to Jamie again. "Ms. Perez, you all accuse me of murder, intimidation, kidnapping, demolition... the list goes on and on," she chuckled. "But, I can trust that you will tell me the truth, right? Have I ever forced you to do anything for me?" Julie had the most deceiving look on her face.

Jamie looked in my direction, as to find the answer of whether she should tell the truth, or lie out of fear.

"I'm right here," Julie stated, blocking Jamie's view of me. "Answer the question,"

"Honestly," Jamie started, "yes. Everything I've done in my life was because of you. I'm tired of being your puppet!" Jamie stated with tears forming in her eyes.

"Name one thing that I've made you do, Jamie. Just one," Julie replied in a whisper.

Jamie did not answer.

"Your Honor, I object," Jared rose to his feet.

"Mr. Hubbard, your staff is objecting quite a bit," Judge Stevens spoke. "Why are you objecting this time?"

"Someone's got to," he replied and there were scattered chuckles across the courtroom.

"Why is it that my client is being pressured the way she is by the defense?" Jared asked.

Judge Stevens did a small eye-roll.

"Overruled. Ms. Perez, we're waiting for an answer," he spoke to Jamie.

"Attempted murder," Jamie stated.

"Attempted murder," Julie repeated. "That's quite the allegation."

Jamie was silent.

"Miss Perez, what's your marital status?" Julie asked.

"I'm in a relationship."

"How are you in a relationship if you are trying to focus on school?" Julie asked her.

"Are you telling me that people don't go to school and enjoy being in a relationship?" Jamie asked her aunt.

"I'm just trying to put 2 and 2 together. Gotta make sure it doesn't equal five, you know?"

Jamie ignored Julie; Julie asked another question.

"How old is your boyfriend?" Julie asked.

I knew exactly where this was going and I nudged Jared.

"Objection, Your Honor! Relevance?" Jared stated.

"Ms. Wilson, where is this going?" the judge asked Julie.

"Your Honor, this is simply trying to identify the witness' background; to verify whether she is a credible source, or not," Julie stated while staring at Jamie.

"But how does asking her significant other's age verify *her* credibility?" Jared argued with Julie.

"Mr. Hubbard, are you upset at something?" Julie smirked.

Jared glared at Julie but didn't reply.

"Overruled, Mr. Hubbard," Judge Stevens spoke after a few seconds. "Ms. Wilson, this better be good," he announced.

"Please answer the question," Julie stated.

"He's 30," Jamie replied after a sigh.

"And, is your boyfriend here today, in this courtroom?" Julie asked, smiling from ear-to-ear.

I knew exactly where this was going.

"Remember, you're under oath," Julie added deviously.

"Yes, he is present," Jamie replied, hesitantly.

"Miss Perez, please identify your boyfriend," Julie finally asked.

As Julie finished the question, my stomach dropped.

"I'm pleading the fifth," Jamie stated.

"Not applicable," the judge answered. "The fifth amendment is used against self-incrimination, Ms. Perez. This is not a situation where the fifth amendment sees fit."

"Come on, Jamie. If he's here, identify him," Julie stated.

Jamie let out a sigh and proceeded to answer. It was clear to her that the judge wasn't about to let up or allow her to not answer the question.

"Richard Young," Jamie stated.

The audience all let out sounds of surprise.

"No further questions, Your Honor," Julie stated before walking back to her seat with a grin.

Abel rose from his seat after a few seconds of silence.

"Your Honor, would the court be willing to grant a short recess?" he asked.

"In light of the new evidence, I will allow it. Court will resume in approximately fifteen minutes, with Ms. Jamie Yvonne Perez on the stand, resuming questioning with the prosecution."

The judge slammed his gavel and Jamie stepped down.

She approached the prosecution's desk but had to pass Julie before reaching us.

"Good luck, Ms. Young— I mean, Perez," Julie whispered with a slight chuckle.

Once Jamie arrived at the desk, Abel spoke.

"Alright guys, so this case has been turned," Abel spoke.

"Julie knew exactly what she was doing," I added as I shook my head.

"And that's exactly why we have to go ten times harder moving forward," Abel spoke. "Jamie's still on the stand, so Jared will be questioning her."

He directed his attention to Jared.

"Ask her about how she's helped the team and her relationship with her aunt." He paused for a moment. "Stay away from any questions that could lead to Richard being mentioned."

"I got it," Jared replied.

"Roberts, don't forget the guy with Julie," I stated.

"The guy has a plan. Regardless of what happens, he's going to try to execute his plan," Abel responded. "We're CPD; we're not going to let that happen."

I nodded my head before stepping away from the desk and walking towards the stand.

I extended my hand and touched the stand; it was cold. As I had my hand on the stand, a vision came to me.

Once I came back to reality, I walked back over to Abel.
***
The judge returned to the courtroom.

Jamie walked back to the stand and Jared followed her.

After she was sworn in, Jared started questioning her.

"Miss Perez, how long have you been assisting the police force?" Jared asked as he slowly paced the floor.

"It's been about 2 or 3 years. I was 25 when I started," Jamie answered.

She kept looking at Julie from her peripheral vision.

"How many interactions have you had with the defendant, also known as your aunt, during this time?" Jared asked.

"About 4."

Jared looked back, as he kept seeing Jamie look at Julie.

Julie displayed a slight smirk.

"Can you do me a favor?" he asked. "Can you start with your very first interaction with your aunt, while you were working for the CPD, and end with the most recent situation?"

Jamie took a deep sigh before starting to explain.

As she explained, I looked in the direction of the man who'd approached us during the lunch recess.

As I focused my attention back on the case, Jared was leaving the stand and was placing Jamie's jacket near the jurors.

Michael rose and walked towards the stand.

"One quick question, Jamie. The necklace around your neck: where'd you get it?" he asked.

"They're really trying it," I whispered to Abel.

Reluctantly, Jamie answered.

"Richard gave me the necklace," she spoke in a low tone.

"Interesting," Michael asked. "Jamie, let me direct your focus to the jacket that was wired. Why was it set up that way and who authorized it?" Michael asked.

Jamie gave him a dirty look before speaking.

"It was to be used to help catch my aunt and I believe Lieutenant Roberts and Detective Young authorized it," she replied.

"Detective Young, or Richard?" Michael asked with a smirk.

Jamie was silent.

"No further questions," Michael returned to his seat.

'Ask her about the bullet wound to her kidney', I wrote on the notepad.

I tapped Jared on his shoulder and tapped the notepad. He read the message and stood back up.

Jared walked back up to Jamie.

"Miss Perez, I have a quick question. During the kidnapping, it is reported that you were shot, correct?" Jared asked Jamie.

"This is correct," she answered.

"Objection, Your Honor," Michael spoke. "Leading the witness."

"Sustained," Judge Stevens spoke.

"I'll reword the question," Jared spoke.

He looked at Jamie and proceeded.

"Miss Perez, when you were buried under the sand, did you suffer from any wounds?"

Michael was silent and Jamie spoke again.

"Yes, I suffered from a gunshot wound ."

"Where were you shot?" Jared asked.

Got 'em, I thought.

"I was shot in the kidney and had to undergo a transplant."

"Would you mind stepping down and showing the jury where you were shot? Just so that they can have an understanding of the wound and where the transplant took place," Jared replied.

Jamie slowly stepped down from the stand and slightly lifted her shirt, exposing the mark that was left behind from when she was shot and had surgery.

The jury looked at the area and released a few gasps.

Jared continued.

"Thank you, Miss Perez," he finished. "No further questions, Your Honor," Jared returned to the desk and I shook his hand.

"Your Honor, I have one rebuttal question for this witness," Michael spoke.

"Go on," Judge Stevens spoke.

"You stated that you had to undergo a kidney transplant," Michael started.

"This is correct," Jamie answered.

"Whose kidney do you have in your body?" Michael asked.

Fuck.

Jamie sighed and spoke with attitude.

"Richard Young's," she spoke.

"Let the record show that much of this evidence is between Richard Young and Jamie Perez," Michael announced. "The fact that they are in a relationship adds to the fact that this may be nothing more than a hoax. Perhaps her kidney failed and she's just using my client to try to cover the expenses of the transplant," he suggested. "I'm just saying, before you say that my client is guilty, take a good look at everything." Michael returned to his seat.

The jury looked at Michael, then to Jamie, and then me.

I finally spoke.

"Your Honor, I would like to call myself to the stand," I stated.

There were more scattered murmurs.

The judge tapped his gavel.

"I see," he widened his eyes. I could tell he was curious as to what I was going to say. "And which of your peers will be questioning you?" he finished.

"I would like to ask for Jamie Perez to do the questioning," I stated.

More noises of shock came from the audience and Abel tapped me.

"Young, what are you doing?" he asked.

"Roberts, we have to make a move that no one is expecting," I replied.

"Well no one is expecting this shit," he whispered to me.

"Trust me on this." I directed my attention back to the judge. "Your Honor, may I?"

"Permission granted," he stated.

I approached the bench, as well as Jamie.

The Deputy swore me in and I sat down.

"Detective Young, how long have you been a part of the Chicago Police Department?" Jamie asked me.

"Approximately ten years," I answered.

"What is your current position in the force?" she asked.

"I'm one of the lead officers of my team," I mentioned. "Not to call myself a boss or anything, but I will say I'm a leader and keep things together," I finished.

"So, it's safe to say you know what you're doing?" Jamie asked.

"That would be correct," I said as I sat erect.

"And, for how many years have you known the defendant, Julie Wilson?"

"I've had interactions with Ms. Wilson for about seven of my ten years with the force."

"Out of all the interactions with the defendant, how many times has she been arrested by your squad?"

"Just once," I replied. "Back in 2008, she was arrested for armed robbery and assault. She was sentenced to seven years but only served three of them. Unless you count the most recent events that landed her in jail," I spoke and I looked over to Julie. "I have to hand it to you, Julie, you're a pretty smart woman and your crimes are well thought out and executed." I started.

"Objection. Your Honor, please tell Detective Young to just answer the question and to not address my client," Michael spoke.

"Sustained," Judge Stevens replied. "Please, stick to the questions, Detective."

I cleared my throat and nodded my head.

"Detective, would you please describe the hostage situation which occurred two years ago, involving Julie Wilson, myself, and multiple Chicago Police officers?"

"Two years ago, the Chicago Police Department was in pursuit of the defendant, Julie Wilson, who was holding yourself, Jamie Yvonne Perez, her niece, hostage."

While explaining the story, Jamie started to tear up.

"We could have sworn we had a lead," I explained. "We traced the ping from your cellphone to New Mexico, but when we arrived at the location, there was nothing there. So, being units that we are," I didn't make it about my effort, "we decided to pull the GPS of the jacket that was entered into evidence. The jacket showed a location in between El Paso, Texas and Ciudad Juarez in Chihuahua, Mexico, so we regrouped and flew there."

Jamie tried her hardest not to let a tear fall from her eye, but she couldn't hold it back any longer.

"When we'd arrived, again, we saw nothing. We were just going off of the location of the jacket. My fellow officers and I searched the land for any disturbed areas. We found a spot that had been interrupted and dug, where we pulled your body from the sand, but the defendant was nowhere to be found. It took an additional two hours to locate Julie Wilson," I concluded.

Abel rose to his feet as more tears streamed down Jamie's face.

"Your Honor, I would like to finish the questioning from this point forward. Allow the victim time to relax."

"Motion denied," Judge Stevens stated.

Abel sat back down and shook his head.

"No further questions, Your Honor," Jamie stated.

As she returned to the desk, Julie approached the bench.

"So, I can't continue the questioning, but Julie can ask questions. What kind of courtroom is this?" Abel whispered to Jared.

"Detective Young; how long have you known me?"

"Roughly 7 years," I stated to her.

"Ouch; that's too long; don't you think?"

"Way too long," I stated. "Especially since every encounter I've had with you has been a bad one," I added.

"So, what recently brought us together?" Julie chuckled as she asked me.

"Would you mind rephrasing the question?" I asked her.

"Dumb it down? Okay," she began. "What is it that you accuse me of this time?"

"Well, accuse means that it is yet to be proven; but we are charging you with kidnapping, robbery, and attempted murder," I spoke.

Julie paced the floor and shook her head.

I looked in the direction of the guy who'd previously threatened us.

"Why do you have it in for me, Detective Young?" Julie continued.

"I should ask you the same question, Ms. Wilson," I replied to her.

"How long have you been attempting to apprehend me?" Julie asked me.

"Ever since your release from prison, Julie. I knew you hadn't changed and were up to no good." I retorted.

"So, it's safe to say you don't trust me?" she smirked.

I thought for a second before proceeding.

"Not just you, Julie." I looked over at Linda. "I don't trust people."

"It is such a shame you feel that way," Julie stated.

I glanced over at the guy; he was dialing numbers on his phone.

"What proof do you have that I have committed such acts?" Julie asked.

"Funny that you should ask me that. We have audio and video footage of you communicating with Jamie, while you had her hostage, as well as assaulting her and making threats," I responded. "With the court's permission, we would like to introduce exhibit C and play the footage for the jury," I stated.

Julie's smile never left her face even after I announced the footage.

"Permission granted. Deputy, please retrieve this footage from the prosecution's desk and commence playback." Judge Stevens remarked.

The deputy retrieved the DVD and inserted it into the player; we were all surprised with what we saw, except for Julie.

Instead of seeing any of the recorded footage, we saw a recording of a children's show.

Abel hung his head as he heard the theme song.

Chuckles came from the audience and the jury let out murmurs.

"Detective Young, is this some kind of joke?" Judge Stevens asked.

"Your Honor, I have no idea how this data ended up on the DVD."

"No further questions, Your Honor," Julie stated with a smirk as she stepped away.

I stepped down from the stand and returned to the desk.

"Do I dare ask anyone to call another witness?" Judge Stevens asked.

"The defense rests, Your Honor," Michael spoke.

"No further witnesses," Abel stated.

Jared nudged him, and Abel looked at Jared.

"What about Linda?" Jared whispered.

"It's no point," Abel replied with a whisper. "It's over, Jared."

"This is not the Abel I know," Jared shook his head. "By any means necessary, right?"

Abel thought for a second before continuing.

"You're right. I got something even better," he spoke to Jared.

Judge Stevens was about to speak again, but Abel interrupted.

"Your Honor, we actually have one more witness that we would like to call to the stand," Abel spoke.

Judge Stevens looked at Abel sternly.

"This is our final witness," he added.

"Proceed," Judge Stevens answered.

"Your Honor, we would like to call Julie Wilson to the stand," Abel projected.

"This should be good," Jared whispered to me.

"Let me handle this," I spoke to Abel.

Julie walked to the stand and was sworn in by the deputy. After sitting down, Julie looked at the prosecution's desk.

"Let's keep this moving," Judge Stevens spoke.

I rose to my feet and Julie smirked. I walked around from the desk and approached her.

"We meet again, Ms. Wilson," I spoke.

"We're always meeting, Detective," she chuckled.

"Ms. Wilson, can you explain your most recent encounter with my unit?" I asked her.

Julie thought for a second.

"All I know is that I was vacationing and on my way back to the city from Oklahoma, and I was stopped by these police officers."

"Did they tell you why you were stopped?" I asked her.

"Something about a kidnapping and attempted murder. They said my niece was shot and buried, and they wanted to question me on the matter," Julie forced her voice to crack.

"And, Ms. Wilson, where did they say your niece was found?" I grilled her.

Julie teared up a little.

"They found her in Texas, near the Mexico border. She was buried under some sand and was shot."

The deputy brought over a box of Kleenex and Julie took one.

You're such a great actor, I thought.

"Please, take your time," I spoke sarcastically.

Julie could tell that I wasn't falling for her tears.

"Thanks," she replied with attitude.

I waited a few seconds for her to finish.

"Ms. Wilson, what is your employment status?" I asked her as I changed the subject.

"I'm currently self-employed," Julie spoke with pride. "I basically do planning for individuals and companies; this is what I'd like to do in the long run," she chuckled.

"Wow, and self-planning makes you money like this?" I asked as I laid a piece of paper with her bank transactions on the desk.

Julie thought as she looked at the paper.

"Well, when you're good at what you do, the money will flow," she slightly smiled.

I decided to try a different line of questioning to attempt to get her tangled in her words.

"Miss Wilson, let's take it back for a moment," I suggested. "I mean, the court already knows, so why not?" I went out on a whim. "When was it that you discovered that your niece and I were dating?"

There were scattered murmurs across the room as I said this.

"What the hell is he doing?" I heard Abel whisper.

A devious grin appeared across Julie's face.

"It was about 3-and-a-half years ago," Julie smiled. "I'm not going to lie to you, I wasn't thrilled to find out that you were dating her."

"And why is that?" I asked as I slowly paced the floor.

"Detective, you locked me away," she chuckled. "I'm not too thrilled that my family member is dating the same police officer who put me behind bars," she shrugged.

"So, you're saying that if I wasn't police, you would be okay with your niece dating me?" I asked.

"You're below our standards," she chuckled.

"Hah," I forcibly laughed aloud. "Is that what you think?" I asked her.

"Objection, Your Honor," Michael called out. "Relevance?"

"Sustained. How does this relate to the trial, Detective?" the judge asked.

"Pardon me, Your Honor," I cleared my throat. "Julie Wilson," I stated as I directed my attention back to her, "is it safe to say that you weren't thrilled to find out that I and your niece were dating because you found out we were working against you?" I asked.

"No," Julie answered.

"Well, you had to have some reason. I am certain it wasn't just a random, hostile reaction."

"I don't have to have a reason to not be thrilled that my niece is dating you," Julie replied as she glanced at Jamie. "Plus," she looked at me, "I told you: you put me in jail, so why would I want my family dating you?"

"Surely you can't control what she does," I replied, "Ms. Perez is a grown woman and is capable of making her own decisions."

"Is that so?" Julie asked.

"Yes," I replied.

"So, if she's capable of making her own decisions, why do you say that she committed crimes because of me?" Julie asked.

"You tell me," I rebutted.

Julie was silent.

"Let me refresh your memory about our most recent encounter," I spoke to Julie. "Something went sideways, and you found out that Jamie was my inside connection."

"I did?" Julie tried to speak.

"You didn't like it, and so you came up with a plan to set me up so that it seemed like I was being unfaithful and she would go back to work with you," I passionately argued.

"Your Honor, objection," Michael spoke aloud.

"And once she went with you, you executed a plan to kidnap and kill her," I spoke.

"Detective," Judge Stevens spoke.

I didn't answer him. I was in a zone and I wanted to get my point across to the jury.

"That isn't the case..." Julie started.

"And then there was a struggle and you shot her. You panicked, and you buried her, thinking you killed her too soon, and you drove away from the scene as quickly as possible."

"He's badgering the witness," Michael spoke.

"Richard!" Abel spoke out.

"And when you found out that she'd survived, you damn near had a heart attack because you knew she would expose you for your crimes," I added.

"Your Honor, control the prosecution," Michael spoke aloud.

"Detective," Judge Stevens spoke louder.

"Those charges are..." Julie's cheeks became red.

"And when the car you were traveling in was impounded, Jamie's prints were found on the trunk and in the backseat; not to add that her phone was found in your car," I finished.

"Detective Young!" Judge Stevens spoke loudly as he banged his gavel.

"Apologies, Your Honor," I spoke.

A few seconds of silence passed before Julie continued.

"I found out that Jamie was dating you, and I wasn't thrilled by it. I felt hurt and betrayed that my family would work against me for no reason," she replied. "I wouldn't have kidnapped my niece and tried to kill her; what would be my motive in doing that?" she asked rhetorically. "Not to mention, that's family, and I wouldn't do anything to hurt my family," she continued. "Yea, I wasn't thrilled, but I didn't try to set you up, and I most certainly didn't call you after the incident at the Hancock Center, and mention that I knew who was working with you, and basically threaten their lives. I wouldn't even mix myself up with that. That isn't the business I conduct."

I knew that I had her wrapped around my finger as I slowly paced the floor. Julie continued speaking.

"What occurred with Jamie was an accident, it just happened; the gun wasn't supposed to go off," she got tangled in her words and the truth slipped out.

She quickly stopped talking after the statement.

I raised an eyebrow as she said this.

Gasps of surprise came from the jury and I felt like I was smiling from ear-to-ear, although I know I didn't let one show.

The jury began to murmur and chat quietly as the confession was revealed. I even saw a look of surprise cross Judge Stevens' face.

"That's funny," I calmly replied. "I said nothing about you calling me or what happened at the Hancock Center," I smirked and walked away from the stand and back to the desk. "And so, you admit to shooting Miss Perez," I projected from the desk.

Julie was completely silent, and her cheeks were a red color.

"No further questions, Your Honor," I sat down in the chair.

***

"Let's wrap this up with closing arguments," Judge Stevens spoke. "Prosecution?"

I rose to my feet and spoke to the jury.

"Many witnesses have been on the stand," I spoke. "It's amazing how the witnesses say the exact same thing about the defendant: she's a cold-hearted, evil, masterminded, criminal. To be honest, Julie has had many opportunities to turn her life around for the better, but she is so obsessed with *my* situation, that she's blind to the fact that she has opportunity," I continued. "The fact that Jamie Perez and myself are in a relationship means absolutely nothing to this case; the evidence should be enough for a 'guilty' verdict, instead of focusing on assumptions. You all have seen with your own eyes the fear that Julie Wilson places on my client, Jamie Perez...."

"Girlfriend," Julie coughed.

"The jury will disregard the remark from the defendant. Another outburst, I will hold you in contempt of court, Ms. Wilson," Judge Stevens spoke.

"My apologies, Your Honor," Julie spoke and cleared her throat.

"Proceed."

I continued my closing argument.

"Jamie Perez fears for her life against Julie Wilson and it isn't a 'respectful' fear, it's a 'save my life' kind of fear. The defendant even admitted to shooting the victim," I reminded them. "I hope you all use all of the evidence shown when reaching a verdict," I walked away from the jury's area and sat down.

Michael rose and walked in front of the jury.

"There have been many witnesses that have said the same thing about my client, but all of that was the past. Ms. Wilson is a changed woman, but the prosecution wants to put her away. Much of the evidence presented has been between Jamie Perez and Richard Young; coincidence?" he suggested. "This whole trial has been planned and is a set-up against Julie Wilson. I really hope you all can see this and notice that no other officer was involved with Ms. Perez, as much as Detective Young was," Michael returned to his seat feeling accomplished.

"Jurors will begin deliberations and court will proceed once a decision is made. The jurors may not discuss this trial outside of this courtroom or deliberation room, and may not let any factors, with the exception of the evidence provided, influence their decision. At the time of announcing their decision, there may not be any outbursts from the audience or anyone on trial," Judge Stevens cleared his throat.

"The unfortunate thing about this case is that misconduct displayed by the prosecution, has been egregious, but because of the nature of the case, I am not going to dismiss it. Miss Wilson deserves a fair trial, just like anyone else," he looked at the prosecution sternly, "and I hope justice can be served, regardless of all of the blatant disrespect set forth."

Judge Stevens hit the gavel against the platform and we all rose to our feet.

He stepped down from the desk and walked into his chambers.

Deputy Thomas walked over to retrieve Julie. He handed her over to another court officer, where he directed her to the holding cell.

The jurors were the next to exit, followed by the defendants, and then the prosecution.

Jared, Abel, myself, and Jamie all regrouped outside.

"What the hell was that?" Abel asked me.

I didn't reply.

"It was completely off-the-top," Abel spoke. "It wasn't by the books at all," he said.

Again, I didn't reply.

"And that's what made it brilliant," Abel finished. "You tied her up, and I think the jury saw that as well."

"By any means necessary, right?" I asked.

I shook Abel's hand and he patted my shoulder before walking in a different direction than I was going.

Jamie, Jared, and I walked down the sidewalk towards the street and we passed the man who had threatened us.

"Didn't we say that Julie had to win? We had a deal," the man stated.

"You know what," Jared started, "you can do what you have to do."

"Say less," he replied.

The man brushed against us and continued walking.
***

An hour later, the judge was notified that the jury had an update. He alerted everyone, and we headed back into the courtroom.

As we re-entered the courtroom, so did Michael, Linda, and Julie's bodyguards.

Deputy Thomas brought Julie into the courtroom and removed her handcuffs. He led her to the Defense's desk.

The jurors entered finally after fifteen minutes.

"I understand that the jury has an update for the court," the judge stated.

"Your Honor, we are unable to reach a verdict in this case. We have attempted, yet there are too many surrounding circumstances to convict Miss Wilson of the said crimes of intended murder, kidnapping, terrorism, arson, or vandalism," juror number one spoke.

"Do you all think that with more time, you would be able to reach a verdict?" he asked.

"No, Your Honor. We are deadlocked."

Judge Stevens slightly shook his head.

"Ladies and gentlemen of the jury, the city of Chicago would like to thank you for your time. If there is nothing further from the jurors, this case is closed. Ms. Wilson will be immediately released and this charge will be wiped from her record. Ms. Wilson, the court apologizes and hopes that you can get back on the right track," The judge stated. "If you are guilty of this or any other crime, hopefully, a more professional prosecution team will be able to bring you to justice in the future, but as of right now, Miss Wilson, you are free to go," he finished and he tapped his gavel.

"All rise!" The deputy spoke, and Judge Stevens exited the courtroom and entered his chambers.

As the people in the crowd left, so did Linda, Julie, and Michael. The other officers, including Abel, started to walk out of the courtroom.

"We'll see you in a moment," I called out.

Abel put a hand in the air and exited the room.

I started to gather my things, as did Jared and Jamie.

"I can't believe this," I spoke as I shook my head.

"We're gonna get her," Jared spoke. "Just a minor setback," he remained optimistic.

I looked and noticed Julie's bodyguards hanging outside of the courtroom. The man looked through the window and noticed the three of us remained in the courtroom.

"I'm going to the bathroom for a second, baby," Jamie spoke as she walked to the door.

"Hurry back," I chuckled. "It's time to get out of here," I did my best to disguise the disappointment I was feeling; not towards her, but regarding the outcome of the case.

Jamie left the room and I continued to talk with Jared.

"Why the hell are they hanging around?" I whispered to Jared.

"I'm not sure, but I don't like this shit one bit," he replied.

"Is Julie still out there?" I asked.

Jared and I both eased over to the door and looked out the window. Julie was nowhere in sight, but we heard quite a bit of commotion outside of the room.

We walked back over to the desk and grabbed our jackets before Jared spoke again.

"It's never a dull moment, huh?" he chuckled as he loaded his weapon.

"Let's handle this shit," I laughed.

We opened the door and followed the sound of the yelling; it was coming from outside of the courthouse.

Jared and I stepped outside and we saw multiple individuals fighting.

'Not today,' I mouthed to Jared and I fired my weapon into the air.

The crowd stopped chanting and the individuals stopped fighting.

I don't feel like this today, I thought.

"Clear out and settle this like adults, ladies and gents," I stated as I showed my badge.

Everyone who was in the crowd scattered and dispersed from the area.

Jamie stepped outside wearing her jacket and had a worried look on her face.

"You set, babe?" I motioned to put my arm around her but she flinched.

A few tears fell from her face.

"What's wrong?" Jared asked.

Jamie slightly unzipped the jacket, and I saw a Velcro strap.

Jared also saw it.

"Baby, unzip the jacket some more," I instructed.

Jared saw the concern on her face.

"Guys, let's move this over here," he motioned for us to move to a corner.

The three of us walked over and Jamie slowly unzipped her jacket, revealing what was underneath.

"If it's not one thing, it's another," Jared stated as he shook his head as he saw the bomb.

"Baby, who did this?" I asked her; I was careful with the contact.

I wanted to embrace Jamie, but I didn't want to potentially trigger the explosive.

She spoke shakily.

"When I walked out to go to the washroom and people started fighting," her eyes became teary, "two men grabbed me, covered my face, and put it on me. By the time I'd removed the sheet from my face, they were gone."

I could tell she wanted to cry.

"Babe, don't cry," I told her. "We don't want to short circuit this bomb or anything.

I looked around and noticed in the distance a guy looking in our direction.

"I see him," I stated as I shook my head. "Jared, you need to fly the helicopter back and I will trail you in the car. Take Jamie with you," I improvised. "This way, I can lead the man away from you all," I stated.

Jared displayed a concerned look.

"The objective would be to take you far away enough that the explosive can't be triggered. I believe it has a range on the remote."

"I hate flying, but let's do it," Jared agreed.

Once we arrived at the helicopter, I programmed it for the airport and started it.
"You sure about this?" Jared asked.
"Yeah, bro. Look, if this goes as planned, he will think that I'm following you, and will follow me. Get up to about 15K!" I yelled over the sound of the propellers.
I left Jared to get into the helicopter.
I ran to my car, drove it to where the helicopter was, and revved my engine.
The engine roars and pops startled the pedestrians and they backed away.

Jared levitated with Jamie until the helicopter wasn't visible.
"Good luck bro," I stated into my radio, which was tuned into the channel of the headset of the pilot.

I looked in my rear-view mirror and saw a guy getting into his car.
"There you are," I spoke aloud. "You want it, here it goes!"
I sped away and the guy followed me.
He tailgated me, and I accelerated more.
Attempting to lose him, I made a U-turn, but it wasn't successful.

I slowed the car down and pulled over. I pulled out my gun as the man slowed down and stopped behind me.
I stepped out of my car and walked towards his. I aimed my gun at him.
"Step out of the vehicle," I demanded.
He rolled up his window and revved his engine.
"Get out of the car," I shouted.

He slowly opened his car door and stepped out.
"Can I help you?" he asked.

"I should be asking you," I replied with attitude. "You've been trailing me since I left the courthouse. Step back," I demanded.

As he obeyed with his hands up, I reached over and pulled the keys out of the ignition and I threw them into the forest next to us.

"You want them, go find them," I stated.

"Come on man, what the f—," he started as he made a motion towards me.

I raised my gun again and he stopped.

"Not today man," I mentioned. "If you want, I can call a tow truck for you," I stated to the man.

I returned to my car and drove to the airport.

I walked inside and saw that Jared and Jamie were sitting on the bench. She kept her jacket closed to not reveal that she had a bomb strapped to her.

I walked over to them and shook my head, but quickly regained my composure.

"Come on, we have to go to the police station," I told them. "Let's get in the car. Let's not make any sudden movements, guys," I told them. "We don't want for this thing to trigger."

We all exited the airport and walked over to my car. I had over a million thoughts racing through my mind; about the bomb, how Julie had just gotten off, and how I was going to deal with her for doing this once I caught back up with her. I managed to divert my attention to the road, and I drove to the police station.

Jared and I walked in and Jamie followed. Anxiety was visible across each officer's face as they saw us enter the building with the bomb on Jamie's chest.

Abel slowly approached the front.
He didn't say a word.
"Julie," I shook my head.
A disgusted look crossed Abel's face.
"Come on," he spoke in a low tone.

He walked us into a steel room, where members of the explosive unit also followed.

I looked around the room and saw the tools on the table to work with the explosives.

"We're going to work in here," the leader spoke as Jared left the room. "Detective, you should get out of here as well," he spoke to me.

"I'm not going anywhere," I spoke as I held Jamie's hand.

The leader saw I wasn't going to back down from my position on this, so he picked up the wire stripping pliers.

He handled the wires carefully as he slowly lifted them to strip the coat of the wires.

I held Jamie's hand tighter and used the Kleenex to wipe her tears and catch them from falling.

"Jamie, I just want you to know, that I love you," I stated to her. "And here, in front of these witnesses, I want to ask you, will you marry me?"

Jamie's eyes widened as I finished the question and immediately replied.

"Yes!" she whispered, trying to fight the tears.

I held her hand tightly as the team member spoke.

"Okay, I'm about to cut," he announced.

Jamie closed her eyes tightly and I tightened my hold on her hand.

15

The light on the explosive went from red to green after the team member cut the wire.

A sigh of relief came from him and Jamie opened her eyes.

"Let's get this off of you," he spoke as he stood to his feet.

I pulled out my utility knife and cut the sides of the vest, creating an opening to remove it from Jamie's body.

The tears flowed down Jamie's face and she repeated her answer louder.

"Yes, I will," she enunciated.

The team member put the explosive in a steel container and exited the room. Jamie and I also stepped into the adjoining room with the other officers.

I got down on one knee and pulled a small box and revealed a ring.

I slid the ring onto her left finger and rose to my feet before embracing her and kissing her.

The officers in the room each applauded this occasion.

After various officers shook my hand and embraced me, Jared approached me.

"Congratulations bro," he extended his hand, grabbed mine, and pulled me in for an embrace. "My bro is finally entering manhood," he chuckled.

"Thanks, bro, but you already know who the best man is going to be," I uttered.

"Who?" Jared asked.

"This nigga," I spoke in a low tone. "You, bro," I chuckled.

"No doubt," Jared replied as he shook hands with Jamie.

Abel walked over and shook my hand.

"Congratulations, Young," he spoke. "I have to admit that I'm extremely proud of everything you've done and I'm ecstatic to have you as a part of this force."

"And I'd like to respond to that with a 'thank you'," I began. "For everything. My first position in law enforcement, trusting my decisions enough to promote me and lead teams; for everything," I finished.

After finishing their congratulations, many officers returned to their offices and cubicles; Jamie and I walked towards the exit of the building.

We exited the building and approached my car.

Jamie walked around to the passenger of the car and opened the door.

Jamie screamed; I looked up and noticed a man standing behind her.

He was holding a knife up to her neck. It was the same person who was following me from the courthouse.

I immediately pulled out my gun, aimed it at him, and turned on my radio so the other officers could hear what was going on.

"Drop your weapon," I shouted over the top of the car.

"Turn off the damn radio!" he demanded.

"Put it down now, let her go!" I stated, ignoring his demand for me to turn off the radio. "Or keep acting all brody, and I'm gonna put a hot one in you."

"Whoa bitch, slow down. You are in no position to be making demands," he stated.

I didn't flinch. I maintained my posture and held the gun firmly.

The man chuckled and made a surface cut on Jamie's hand. She started to bleed.

Officers heard the transmission and emerged from the police station, all of them aimed their guns at the man.

"Young, it's your call," Abel shouted as he aimed his weapon; this is something I rarely saw him do.

"Look around," the man chuckled. "You guys won't win this round," he smirked.

Many masked gunmen appeared from the vantage points on top of nearby buildings with machine guns and sniper rifles. Some of the men aimed their weapons at police officers, but most of them had the firearms aimed at me.

"Julie?" I questioned.

"Now you know better than to ask me for some names," the man spoke. "This Chicago, nigga," he laughed. "Snitches and bitches get stitches," he never moved the knife from Jamie's neck.

"Ricky," Jamie cried softly.

"Drop your gun, Pig. Send your people inside," the man demanded.

"Return to base," I surrendered, but I never lowered the gun. "Don't worry about me, just return inside," I stated to them.

"Is he serious right now?" a fellow officer spoke.

"Let's just do what he says," another officer replied.

The situation had escalated at this point, and I know there was going to be some bloodshed before this was over.

I glanced over my shoulder and saw the look that Jared gave me; I knew he was about to pull a stunt.

Jared walked inside with the rest of the officers.

"Okay, Officer, now slide your gun over here," he mentioned.

I didn't want to risk Jamie's life any more than it already was, so I followed his instructions.

"Look man, just don't hurt my fiancé," I surrendered.

"So, I guess we're having a small celebration here — a going away party." The man chuckled and continued to speak, "I never leave a job undone."

I heard the guns being loaded by the multiple men on top of the buildings, and the man picked up my gun and aimed it at me while keeping his hold around Jamie.

Jared emerged from the building with an ammunition belt, filled with ammunition and smoke grenades.

He threw a handful of smoke grenades near the vehicle and they all exploded, filling the area with smoke.

"Kill that fool," the man shouted; he couldn't see, but he did his best to take cover while holding onto Jamie.

I heard him scream and panic, as I stayed low to the ground. Jamie crawled around to my side of the car and I could hear Jared's gunfire getting closer to us.

I opened the driver's door and Jamie crawled inside and over the gear selector' to sit in the passenger's seat. I got in behind her and quickly started the vehicle.

I revved the engine, which caused a few pops to emit from the exhaust, and the men on the roof shot at the vehicle.

With bullets flying all around, I put on my bright lights as well as my fog lights and drove over to Jared. He got into the back of the vehicle while alternating his shots between the man and the men on the roof.

I drove off and made a wide turn at the corner and Jared stopped shooting the gun.

"Jared, you are all kinds of crazy!" I shouted while still driving and holding Jamie's hand.

"You're my bro and I told you I had your back no matter what. I plan on keeping my word," he answered.

"My boy," I replied as he patted my shoulder.

I directed my attention towards Jamie.

"Baby, are you okay?" I asked her.

"I'm just a little scared, Ricky," she stated.

"Jared, look under your seat and pass me that towel for Jamie," I mentioned.

As Jared passed me the towel, I called to the police station on my radio.

"Lock it down; I am unharmed and uninjured, but the shooter is still out there. Armed and dangerous."

"10-4, Young," Abel spoke. "We've already eliminated some of the threats on top of the buildings, and we have backup en route," he replied.

I turned the radio down and continued to drive.

"Jamie, I'm going to drop you off at Jared's," I spoke. "I have to go back and make sure this situation is handled."

"And what about me?" Jared chuckled.

"See, I would take you back, bro," I chuckled, "but I need for you to stay home and make sure Jamie, Madison, and Jacob are all okay. It's too much going down right now," I finished.

"I get you," Jared replied.

"Okay, baby," Jamie spoke. "You gotta do what you gotta do."

I drove to Jared's house and I let Jamie out. Jared exited the vehicle behind her.

He shook my hand and walked to the house and opened the door.

Jamie stood at the car door and leaned over.

"I love you, baby," she mentioned to me.

"I love you, too, babe," I replied.

She placed her lips on mine and we kissed. She retreated and tapped on the car before walking inside.

I drove away from Jared's house and back towards the police station.

I drove around to the back entrance of the building, where I had a visual of everyone.

As I got out of the car, I walked into the back door of the police station. I rushed over and retrieved a sniper rifle before returning outside.

I ran up the fire escape, so I could have a good vantage point. I took my post and lied down, looking through the scope of the sniper.

I aimed the gun at one of the shooters and I prepared to fire the first bullet. As I was about to pull the trigger, I felt the muzzle of a gun press against the back of my head.

"Think about it," the man spoke.

I put my hands up and released the trigger. I slowly rose to my feet.

"I've been waiting a long time for this," he stated.

I turned slightly and observed the man standing behind me.

"What's the vendetta with me?" I asked him.

He didn't answer, and I heard the gun cock.

I heard a piercing shot; I turned and saw the man falling to the ground with a bullet through his chest.

As his body hit the ground, the gun slid to the edge of the rooftop, near the gutter.

Linda stood with a gun extended.

I slowly walked over to Linda.

She reached out for a handshake and I hugged her.

She was silent during the ordeal.

I took the gun from her hands as I silently thanked her for saving my life.

Abel ran to the rooftop where Linda and I were located. He cleared his throat as he saw the embrace.

"What is this?" Abel asked as he had his weapon drawn and slowly walked over to us.

"She just saved my life, Roberts," I told him.

I pointed to the suspect.

"We're good?" I spoke calmly as I made eye contact with her.

She slightly nodded her head to confirm.

More officers came up the staircase, and one walked towards the deceased suspect. Abel walked over to the man with the other officers.

He called my name and I walked over to him.

"Do you recognize him?" Abel asked me.

"He put the bomb on Jamie and followed me from the courthouse," I spoke with a look of disgust on my face. "I know he's affiliated with Julie, but I don't know him personally," I finished.

"That explains some of it, he came to kill Jamie, but since she's not here..."

"He tries to kill the closest thing to her — me," I finished his sentence.

As we spoke, the officers began to pat down the deceased suspect. He pulled an ID out of the pocket and reason the name aloud.

"James Kingston," the officer read from the man's ID.

"James Kingston... I've heard that name before," I stated to Abel. "Roberts, Linda: come with me," I mentioned as I rushed downstairs.

Abel and Linda both followed behind me; paramedics were arriving on the scene to treat the wounded and to pick up the deceased.

We all walked into my office. I turned on the computer and logged in. I typed 'Kingston, James' into the search field.

A result appeared, and I clicked on the name. A full profile of the man was populated on the screen.

"James Kingston: 30 years old, 2 children, married." I read. "No priors."

"Young, what does this have to do with anything?" Abel asked.

"Listen to this. Former occupation: Detective of CPD: Unit 52. Affiliations: Julie Wilson."

Abel looked at me with concern.

"Alias: Michael Wilson," I finished.

16

"So, Kingston was one of our own. And he went by the name 'Michael Wilson'. That's Julie's cousin," Abel stated.

"Well, it damn sure didn't look like him," I mentioned. "But then again, it's an alias, so one of the names isn't correct," I finished.

"Maybe 'Michael' isn't who he says he is," Linda suggested.

I could tell she was trying to earn my trust, but I wasn't going for her antics.

"This is possible, but we need motive," I entertained her idea. "This has opened a brand-new case. He could have been a U-C," I stated.

"Well, let's put this on hold for now," Abel stated as he pressed the red icon on his phone. "I just got a report of a disturbance at Officer Hubbard's home."

"What the hell?!" I spoke.

"I know," Abel continued. "Let's ride, Young. Linda, you're coming with us," Abel finished.

It was obvious he was still suspicious of her arrival.

"We're taking two cars," he added. "We're going to attack from two different directions."

"Sounds like a plan to me," I spoke.

We left the office and got into our vehicles.

Linda rode with me in my car, and Abel decided to drive a standard police car.

"Ricky, Julie may be over there," Linda suggest as I drove.

"What do you mean?" I questioned as I accelerated.

"Julie has been the brains behind every operation so far; finding out where you and Jamie would go would be nothing to her."

"Roberts, I've just received notice that Julie may be at Jared's. We have to proceed with caution," I announced over my radio.

"The element of surprise," he replied. "Let's shut her down, now," Abel spoke and I could hear him accelerate.

"10-4," I replied before returning the receiver to the pocket.

Linda put her head down and started to place her hands in her pockets.

"Keep your hands on your lap, Linda," I instructed.

My suspicion grew as Linda had just released this new information about Julie to me.

We arrived at Jared's home, and I noticed that the door was wide open.

"Linda, you are to stay here," I demanded as I locked one handcuff on her right hand and the other to the steering wheel.

"Is this really necessary?" she chuckled.

"With you?" I looked at her. "Yes," I secured the cuff.

I closed the car door and walked to Jared's front door, followed by Abel.

I made eye contact with him and pulled out my gun. We both walked into the home.

"Jared," I called out as Abel and I looked around the room.

I didn't get a response.

"Jamie," I called out; no answer.

I heard footsteps and I turned around. I saw a figure behind Abel.

"Roberts, watch out!" I shouted.

He quickly shifted his body and I fired a bullet at the figure.

The bullet missed, and the suspect started to run through the house and into a dark room.

Abel and I ran behind the suspect into the room, and we saw Jared sprawled out on the bed.

Jamie was nowhere to be found, neither was the suspect.

Abel noticed an open window and looked out of it as I walked up to Jared.

"The suspect is gone," Abel spoke as he radioed back to the station.

"Jared," I whispered as I shook him.

He didn't respond.

I saw a water bottle on the floor next to me and I picked it up. I poured the water on his face and shouted his name.

He quickly jumped up using his hands to defend himself.

"Woah, Jared, calm down," I spoke as I tried to bring him back to reality.

"What the hell happened? Where's Julie?" Jared asked as he calmed down.

"Julie?" Abel asked as he heard her name.

"What do you remember?" I asked him.

"Julie entered and... The bitch hit me with her pistol and Jamie... Wait, where is she?" he asked looking around.

"No sign of her or Julie," I stated.

I stood up and paced back and forth, taking deep breaths. I turned quickly and punched the wall; I feared the worst.

"Richard!" Abel shouted as he and Jared walked over to me, both grabbing my arms to calm me down.

"Let me go!" I shouted, as I pulled my arms away and pulled out my gun.

"Stop, bro!" Jared and Abel managed to sit me on the bed. "I promise you we will get Julie and be done with this shit for good! We just need to keep our heads."

"To hell with everything else!" I retaliated. "My focus right now is to get Jamie back and... Oh shit!" I stated as I quickly rose from the bed to my feet.

I ran out of the room and Jared realized what was going on and ran behind me. Abel followed.

"Madison!" I called out as I power-walked towards her and Jared's room. "Jared, where's Jacob?" I shouted to him.

"He was with Madison taking a nap. Check her room, I'm gonna check the basement," Jared spoke as he and Abel ran down the staircase.

I quickly opened Madison's door. She and Jacob both appeared to be asleep on the bed.

"Madison," I called, trying to wake her up.

There was no movement from her or Jacob.

The closer I got to them, the more they appeared to be lifeless.

"No, no, no, no, no," I exclaimed. "Abel, Jared, call a bus!" I shouted. Jared and Abel both ran upstairs to the room.

"Jared, I'll take Jacob and perform CPR on him, while you work on Madison. Roberts, call 9-1-1 and get an ambulance over here ASAP."

Jared walked over to his wife as I began to gently press on the infant's chest.

He began CPR on his wife and I held Jacob over my shoulder, keeping his head up and massaging his back, desperate to get a pulse.

I breathed into his mouth while closing his nose and he started to breathe; a pulse finally came about.

The baby started to cry. I held him close to me and kissed him on the forehead. I looked over to Jared, but Madison was still lifeless.

Abel stood at the door as the paramedics arrived, minutes later. They rushed in and put Madison on the stretcher.

They put an oxygen mask on her and inserted an IV in her arm.

Jared let the tears roll down his face and I passed Jacob to him.

He held Jacob tight and we walked outside to check on Madison.

"We got a pulse!" The paramedic shouted to the others.

Madison was now breathing, yet her eyes were still closed. Jared walked closer and held Madison's hand. Jacob then started to reach down for his mother, and uttered the words, "Mama."

Jared knelt so the baby could touch Madison's hand and upon the touch of his hand, she closed her hand on his and opened her eyes.

Jared held Madison's hand tighter and kissed her on the forehead. "Thank you, Lord," he whispered.

I put my hand on his shoulder and wiped the few tears that accumulated in my eyes.

Neighbors had gathered outside to see what was happening.

"Ricky, you better find this bitch before I do!" Jared exclaimed. "I swear I'm gonna kill her," Jared stated while still holding Madison's hand.

I motioned my hands to quiet Jared down in case there were any cameras around.

"I gotta find Jamie," I started. "Julie is done with once I find her."

"Let's all calm down for a minute," Abel started. "No one's going to die if we can help it," I assumed it was his uniform speaking, as I could see the anger in his eyes. "I promise you that we will follow every protocol possible to ensure this is dealt with."

"Abel, this shit just got personal. She came into my home and almost killed my wife and son. Forget the fact that she assaulted me. I promise you, someone's going down," Jared growled.

One of the paramedics that were tending to Madison tapped me on the shoulder.

"Officer," he started.

"Detective Young," I told him as I reached for a handshake.

He shook my hand and continued.

"We have done blood work and we're going to test it and notify you of the results. Protocol is to take her back to the hospital with us, but personally, everything seems okay. She seems healthy and not ill by any of the common poisons. Why rack up medical expenses, you know?" he asked. "Is she the only victim?"

"No, she's not the only one. The baby was also a victim, but we were able to perform CPR and get him back," I mentioned. "I think you may want to talk to the husband about what to do," I further suggested

Jared stood beside me and heard the whole conversation.

He handed the paramedic the baby and proceeded to speak.

"You're right. Let her stay home and inform us of the results as soon as you find out anything. No need to accrue extra bills," he chuckled.

"Will do. Let's get some blood from the infant," the paramedic stated to the others.

They adjusted the gurney, so Madison could sit up and removed her oxygen mask. Jared followed the paramedic with Jacob and I started to talk to Madison.

"Madison, what do you remember?" I gently asked her.

"I don't remember much," she started. "All I remember is seeing and wrestling with Julie to protect Jacob."

"So, there's a chance that you scratched her," I suggested.

"Possibly," Madison spoke. "I can't quite recall," she admitted. "She was wearing gloves and her skin was completely covered."

"Abel, Madison may have Julie's DNA under her fingernails," I called. "Let's get forensics over here."

The paramedics took a swab from under her fingernails and put the q-tip in a sealed bag.

Jared walked back over to us holding the crying infant.

"Can I hold my baby, please?" Madison asked.

Jared handed Jacob to Madison and the baby seemed to immediately cease crying.

Jacob was still fussing, so Madison gave him her finger and he started to play with it.

"Rick, look." Madison pointed behind me and I turned around.

Jamie was walking towards us with a bloody shirt; tears were falling from her eyes.

"Jamie," I stated and walked up to her.

Upon reaching her, I embraced her.

She hugged me tightly and cried silently.

"What happened, baby?" I asked her.

"I fought my aunt and ran. She's looking for me, babe."

"I got something for that ass," Jared stated and pulled out his handgun. "Where is she, Jamie?"

"No, you don't have anything yet," Abel spoke. "We are going to hang back, and let Julie come to us," he planned.

"Yeah, the people we care about most are okay. That's all that matters," I responded, using one of my hands to lower his gun. "Are you hurt, babe?" I asked her.

"I'm not hurt, majorly; just a few scratches, but I am scared for my life. For the first time, she held a gun to my throat."

"Baby, you're with me now and you're going to stay with me. I'm not leaving you alone," I stated.

Jamie hugged me tighter, and I kissed her forehead.

Moments later, the paramedics helped Madison off of the gurney and to her feet. She walked over to Jared and grabbed his hand.

The paramedic returned to speak.

"Alright, Detective. Whoever did this is definitely no amateur. While Mrs. Hubbard and the infant seem to be okay, the woman knew exactly how to cleanly execute this. You may want to keep an eye out," he suggested.

"You have no idea," I stated to him.

We shook hands and he walked off.

As the paramedics packed up and drove off, we all re-entered Jared's home.

"Come here, Mami, let me look at you," I stated to Jamie.

Upon reaching me, I pulled her in and hugged her tightly.

Abel walked over to the door and put his right hand up. This was one of the first times it seemed like the case was too much for him.

"Young, take the rest of the day off and tomorrow if needed; same to you Hubbard," Abel spoke. "Let's get Linda back to the police station and then we'll pick this back up tomorrow."

"Jared, you and Madison come with us. I'm going to have you all sleep over at my house. I can't imagine what I would do if something were to happen to either of you," I stated.

Jared and Madison both packed some clothes, got some things ready for Jacob, and we left their house.

I opened the driver's door and climbed inside. Jared, Madison, Jamie, and Jacob climbed into the back seat.

"Is everything okay?" Linda asked.

"Wouldn't you like to know?" I spoke as I unlocked the handcuff.

"Don't do that, Ricard," Linda spoke softly. "You just had me out here handcuffed for two hours, and you're giving me attitude?"

"Don't start with me, Linda," I looked at her sternly before driving off.

Jared, Madison, Jamie, and Jacob were all silent as they watched on.

As we drove back to the police station, there was complete silence, until I spoke again.

"Linda, you're going to remain in the police station until we figure everything out," I never took my eyes off the road.

"I'm sorry about everything, Rick," Linda stated.

"What do you mean?" I asked as I glanced at her.

She then pulled a gun out and aimed it at me.

I quickly lowered my left hand to my side with my right hand on the steering wheel.

"Don't do that," she suggested.

I slowly lifted my hand and returned it to the steering wheel.

"Pull the car over, and the rest of you better keep your hands where I can see them, or else we will all die right here."

I pulled the car over and obeyed Linda's demands.

"Take out the keys and give them to me," Linda demanded while aiming the gun at my head.

As she demanded the keys, a transmission came through the radio.

"Roberts to Young, I notice that you haven't arrived at the station yet. Is everything okay?" Abel asked.

Linda demanded that I turn off the radio; I obeyed in turning off the radio, but I didn't turn off the car.

She pushed the gun against my head and told me to turn off the engine and to give the keys to her.

I slowly removed the keys from the ignition and passed them to Linda.

She snatched the keys away and ordered everyone to get out of the car. As we all exited, Jamie accumulated tears in her eyes and ran towards me. Once she reached me, I kissed her on the forehead and hugged her.

"Madison, cover Jacob's ears. When I move my left leg, I want you to get down," Jared whispered.

"I guess it's 2 for the price of one," Linda stated as she aimed the gun at Jamie and me.

I positioned myself in front of Jamie and lifted my chin.

"Go on and do it, Linda. You have that gun out for a reason, right?" I mentioned.

Fear filled my whole body, but I didn't dare to show it.

"You think you're tough now?" Linda started. "Oh, what, so you get a bitch, and then you grow some balls?" Linda asked.

Jamie ran from behind me and tried to attack Linda.

"Jamie, don't," I mentioned grabbing her arm.

"No, let the bitch through. Let's see what she's going to do!" Linda challenged.

"You are a sick and deranged individual, Linda," I looked in the direction of Jared and Madison. "Let me kiss my people goodbye if you want to waste me."

"Eh, I guess that shit wouldn't hurt. You got half a minute."

Jamie and I eased past Linda over to Jared and Madison. I asked to hold Jacob.

As they handed me the baby, he cooed and played with my finger and giggled.

"You're too young to understand, Jacob, but I love you nephew," I looked up. "Jared, Madison; I love you all with all of my heart, and please take good care of Jamie for me."

"I love you, Richard," Madison stated and kissed me on the cheek.

She reached for Jacob and I passed him to her.

Jacob started to cry as he left my arms. Madison gently bounced him to soothe him.

"Jamie, I wish I could have you alone just one more time," I mentioned to her.

I kissed her passionately and she began to cry.

"I love you mami, don't cry."

We embraced one last time and I released.

I walked over to Jared for a handshake.

"Keep your head up and leading the force," I spoke.

He gave me a handshake and uttered, "I got you."

As he said the words, I knew he was up to something.

I took off my chain and put it around Jacob's neck. "It's a little big, but you'll grow into it," I chuckled.

"Alright, this family time has to end. Get over here," Linda demanded.

Madison put her hands on Jamie's shoulders and held her back as I walked back over to Linda; she whispered in Jamie's ear.

"Alright, Linda, since you pulled the piece out on me, you have to use it," I spoke as I repositioned myself.

Linda prepared to pull the trigger.

I made eye contact with Jared, and he moved his left leg. Madison got on the ground and covered Jacob's ears and Jamie got down next to her.

Before Linda pulled the trigger, Jared pulled out his gun and fired one bullet. It hit Linda in the back of the head and she started to fall.

I saw Linda fall to the ground with a bullet to the head; blood was rushing from her brain. I immediately felt parts of my head and torso to determine if I was hit: I wasn't.

"Ricky!" Jamie exclaimed and ran over to me.

I picked her up and by now she was crying full tears.

She began to kiss me all over my face.

"I love you so much, baby, and I was scared that I was going to lose you."

"I'm right here, Jamie," I stated to her before I looked over to Jared.

He walked over to me and reached out for a handshake.

I took his hand in mine and hugged him.

"What about aiming low?" I asked him with a chuckle.

"That therapy shit don't always work, bro," Jared laughed.

Madison walked over to me and gave me Jacob. She wiped her tears as Jacob played with my fingers.

Madison hugged Jared as he put his gun away and I pulled Jamie close to me and Jacob.

"Hello, Abel," Jared spoke over his phone. "Yeah, we're going to need a bus over here on 18th and Cicero," he announced. "Suspect down," Jared finished before hanging up.

Jamie kissed Jacob on the cheek and held my hand tightly.

Paramedics soon arrived on the scene and put Linda on a stretcher. They covered her body and started to wheel her over to the ambulance.

"Hold on, for a second," I mentioned to one of the paramedics.

I reached into Linda's pockets and grabbed my keys to the car. "I don't think we'll be seeing you again, Linda," I stated before walking away.

We all returned to the car and I turned on my radio to let inform Abel as to what was going on and to request that he send an officer back to the crime scene.

Abel sent an officer back to the scene, and once the officer arrived, I changed directions and drove home.

17

Later that night, Jared, Madison, and Jacob were in their room. Silence filled the home.

Jamie lied down next to me with her head on my bare chest.

Occasionally, she would look up at me; when I would make eye contact with her, she would look away.

"Come here, babe," I told her as I had her straddle me. "Talk to me. What's troubling you?" I asked her.

She looked down at me and interlocked our fingers.

"Daddy, I've just had an incredibly rough day. I've been strapped with a bomb, had guns aimed at me, and worst of all, I almost lost you today."

"And all of this happened on the same day as Julie's trial," I shook my head. "Baby, but we're okay. I'm not going to let anything happen to you. I promise," I assured her.

"But baby, what if Linda did pull the trigger and," Jamie started before I put my finger to her lips.

"Baby, don't speak of Linda," I stated to her in a soft tone.

I saw that she was upset, so I continued.

"What can I do to make you feel better?" I asked her.

She let out a sigh and thought.

"Love me, Daddy," she stated in a soft tone.

"Baby, let me get the..."

She pushed me back down.

"No. I want to have your child," she added seductively.

I looked up at her and she bent down and gave me a passionate kiss.

"Make love to me," she added.

She kissed my neck while running her hands down my chest.

A bolt of strength shot through my body, and I rose to my feet while holding her; her arms were around my neck, and her legs were wrapped around my waist. I walked over to the door while holding her, and she reached one hand around and locked it.

She returned her arm to my neck and I walked back over to the bed.

I laid her on the bed, slowly spreading her legs apart while looking into her eyes. The very touch of her skin against mine turned both of us on and it increased our body temperatures, making the room seem steamy and feel like a sauna.

I kissed down her stomach and around her naval; I could tell this was her sweet spot.

"*Ay, Papi... Damelo*" she stated in between her heavy moans.

We made sure not to make too much noise and we continued our intimate, romantic session.

***

The next morning, I awoke and saw Jamie lying next to me. The worst seemed to be behind us, for now.

I got up and walked to the washroom.

I turned on the faucet and listened to the water run for a few seconds before retrieving my toothbrush from the drawer.

I brushed my hair and my teeth, as I let the thoughts of Julie and Linda pass through my mind.

But I wasn't upset. Part one of the two-part problem was no more; it was time to refocus and keep my vision.

As I returned to my room and closed the door, there was an immediate knock.

I cracked the door and saw Jared wearing a white tee, basketball shorts, and a du-rag.

I eased out of the door and closed it behind me.

"Put a shirt on bro," he mentioned to me with a chuckle.

I wasn't wearing anything but my gym shorts.

"Good morning to you, too," I chuckled.

"So, let me know... How was it?" he questioned; I knew what he was referring to.

"Shit's personal," I replied.

"Oh, she has you on lockdown?" Jared laughed and hit me in the arm.

"Nah, it's not even like that. Do you know who I am?" I questioned with a smirk.

"Yea, whatever," he stated. "Shit was crazy yesterday."

"It was way too much that went down. Julie's case, the bomb strapped to Jamie, the shootout, witnessed two deaths, and I would have lost my damn mind if I would have lost you, Madison, and-or Jacob," I confessed.

"Yeah, I get you bro," he started "but we're good. And I'm going to make sure we keep it that way. Oh," he undid the tie to his du-rag, "and don't even worry about Julie," he finished.

"I'm not worried about her," I spoke as I adjusted the strings to my shorts.

I glanced back at the clock before continuing.

"Let me go make my bride-to-be some breakfast before she wakes up," I stated to Jared.

"Oh damn," he chuckled. "She's got you sprung out," he laughed, heartedly.

"Yea, nigga," I started, "*you* wish," I punched him in the arm as we both walked down the stairs and made our way to the kitchen.

After I finished, Jared made his way back to his room and I put the food on a table and carried it upstairs. As I opened the door, Jamie slowly woke up.

"There's my bride," I stated with a smile. "How'd you sleep, baby?" I asked.

"Don't even ask," she chuckled.

"Well, I don't have to," I slightly laughed. "These scratches on my back say that you slept pretty well," I added as I walked over to the bed and I placed the table over her lap.

I climbed into the bed and lied next to her.

"Don't be a little bitch about it," Jamie chuckled. "What's this?" she asked, seemingly surprised at the breakfast that I'd prepared for her.

"I decided to make my bride some breakfast," I started. "Here you have eggs Florentine, with a few turkey sausage links on the side, and two pancakes to give you energy from last night; syrup on the side, of course," I joked.

She jokingly punched me in the arm.

"What are you trying to say?" she laughed.

"Nothing at all, baby," I chuckled. "I just didn't know how much syrup you wanted."

"Uh-huh," she spoke as she rolled her eyes.

"And, a glass of orange juice to wash all of that down," I finished.

"And what's for dessert?" she asked, seductively.

"Dessert in the morning?"

"Come here," she whispered.

I leaned in and Jamie put her lips against mine. What started as a regular kiss, was now an erotic and fiery explosion.

"Now *that*, was some sweet desert," she smiled when we retreated from the kiss.

"Why don't you give me a little more desert, babe?" I suggested.

She thought for a second and displayed a focused look on her face.

"I would," she spoke a few seconds later with a chuckle, "but I am pretty sure that I hear a little one downstairs. Plus, I am exhausted from last night," she added.

"Well, eat up, Mami. Let's get your energy back," I chuckled.

I started to feed Jamie and pamper her.

As she finished eating her food, we laid there for a moment before getting up.

She put on a pair of sweat pants, put her hair in a ponytail, and got out of bed. She went to the washroom to wash-up and brush her teeth. Once she finished, I put on a shirt and I carried her on my back down the stairs.

"Hey, let's wake Madison and Jared up," I whispered to Jamie.

She knew I wanted to do something childish, so she emitted a small chuckle before walking with me to the closet.

We pulled out small water pistols and filled them with water.

"You go in first, Jamie," I told her as we eased to their door.

We peered our heads into the room and entered; we saw Jared with his arm wrapped around Madison in bed. Madison held Jacob close to her as they all slept.

I counted down from three to Jamie and as she shot her pistol at Jared and Madison, I shot mine at her.

She was shocked that I'd just shot the water-gun at her as opposed to Jared and Madison, yet she started laughing.

Jared and Madison were now awake because of the water that Jamie sprayed on them.

"You dog," she stated with a laugh as she started to spray water in my direction.

Jared released Madison and rose to his feet. Madison got up with Jacob, and she and Jared moved around to avoid the water.

As we all played in the water, we did not hear the doorbell ring; however, we heard sirens accumulate outside.

"Hold on, y'all," I stated as the lights caught my attention.

I walked to the window, where I saw many police vehicles. "Jared, come with me," I told him.

As we approached the door, we saw Abel walking to my porch.

"Roberts, what's going on?" I asked him as I opened the door.

"I didn't get a reply from you all over the radio, so I gathered the gang and we came over," Abel spoke.

"Sorry about that, Abe," Jared spoke. "Didn't have the radio turned on. It was a long night."

"It's okay," Abel replied. "There's been a disturbance reported at Michael Wilson's home."

"Michael Wilson or James Kingston?" I asked, skeptically.

"Whoever he may be, we have to get over there now!" Abel concluded.

"Okay, cool," I started. "Well you all get a head start; Jared and I will be over there as soon as we throw on some clothes."

"Hurry it up," Abel stated before turning around and walking down the steps.

Jared and I both went to one of the bathrooms in my home and took showers and got dressed. When we finished, we both walked back to the room where Jamie and Madison were playing with Jacob.

"Jamie, Madison, we gotta go; we'll be back," I mentioned to them as Jared stood by my side.

"What's wrong, Rick?" Jamie asked me.

"Something's come up and Jared and I have to go over your cousin's house," I answered. "But before we go, I want to ask you a question."

"Ask me anything."

"Who is 'Michael Wilson?'" I asked.

"What do you mean?" Jamie appeared to be confused.

"The guy who tried to kill you yesterday," I started, "his name was James Kingston, but his alias was Michael Wilson," I explained as I closed the holster to my weapon and ensured it was secure on my side.

"The only Michael Wilson that I'm familiar with is my cousin."

"What about Kingston?" I asked.

"All I know is that Michael and James are, well, they were good friends. I've always known my cousin to be Michael Wilson. I never knew they used the same alias," Jamie mentioned.

"Bro, come on, we gotta go," Jared stated.

"Jamie, we'll be back. Hold it down till I get back baby; you know where the protection is," I stated to her.

"I know, Daddy," she added.

I kissed her goodbye and Jared kissed Madison before we both left out of the house.

**

"What do you think is going down?" Jared asked as I turned down Michael's block.

"I haven't the slightest clue," I spoke as I shook my head. "I just hope it's nothing too crazy. Abel looked like he was in a frenzy when he showed up."

"Fingers crossed," Jared spoke.

The closer we drove to Michael's home, the more difficult it became to navigate due to the emergency vehicles and civilians on the road.

"Looks like we're getting out right here Jared," I mentioned; Michael's home was on the next block but there wasn't any way that we were going to get there with the car.

"I wonder what happened," Jared stated as he got out of the car and pulled out his gun.

"We'll find out soon enough. Fingers crossed, right?" I remarked while closing my door and locking it.

We both walked over to Michael's home. We held our badges so that they were visible, and the other officers would let us through.

"Roberts, what's the situation?" I asked him as Jared and I reached the steps to Michael's home.

"He's dead, Young."

"Dead?" I questioned.

"A single bullet to the heart. Examiners say he was shot, was able to reach a phone and dial 9-1-1, and died minutes, later," Abel shook his head in disgust.

"I guess Chicago's emergency personnel responded too late," Jared stated.

I was in disbelief, but I knew at that exact moment who was responsible.

"I have a feeling that I know who's responsible," I spoke as I looked around.

"We have to leave that woman alone," Abel spoke as he knew who I was referring to. "Until we get some hard evidence, you both are ordered to stay away from her," he finished.

"Understood," I reluctantly responded.

"I don't want to take on this case, Roberts," I added moments later.

"You won't have to," Roberts stated. "You and Jared can do the desk work. We'll assign the heavy lifting to another officer."

"I sense a vacation," Jared joked.

"Desk duty," Abel reiterated with a slight chuckle.

"Now you already know that we don't belong behind a desk, Abe," Jared answered. "We gotta be where the action is. But my boy doesn't want to handle this specific case. Can't we work something out?" he finished.

"It's okay, J," I said. "What do you need to me do, Roberts?" I asked.

Abel studied my body language and the expression on my face.

"Nah, you know what, Hubbard's right. Young, you don't have to take this case. Take a week or two off, paid leave, and get your mind right."

Jared cleared his throat.

"Take this S-O-B with you," he joked. "So that I won't have to be bothered," Abel chuckled. "The rest of us are going to finish here."

"Thanks, Roberts," I responded as I shook his hand.

Jared also shook his hand before we walked down the steps.

We started to walk back to my vehicle before I spoke again.

"I'm gonna get Jamie and go somewhere that nobody knows our name. She doesn't need to hear this about her cousin." I added.

"She's gonna find out eventually," Jared spoke.

"Yea, I know. But let me be the one to tell her," I reluctantly uttered.

I unlocked the door and Jared got into the passenger's side.

"Bro, I'm proud of you. I know I may not tell you on a daily, or show it, but I've watched you grow and become the man you are today," Jared stated.

"What's making you say this?" I asked him.

"I just want you to know. It's true though. I know I'm not perfect and, honestly, I want Jacob to be someone like you. Acts like me, but thinks and behaves like you," Jared chuckled.

"That's love, bro," I told him as I drove off.

"How's Jamie been treating you?" Jared asked.

"You see how we are. We may argue or disagree, fuss and fight, but she's my queen, and shit, I don't know, I try to be her king," I mentioned.

"I'm sure you are. Man, you're her rock. I've seen the way you all are together." Jared added.

"I try to be," I started. "I don't know what I would do if I were to lose her or if something were to happen to her. That's why I tell her every day how much she means to me."

Jared listened as he unloaded his weapon.

"I don't want to live with regrets; the next moment isn't promised," I continued. "I can't live life wishing there was something I could have done to prevent certain situations or things I should have said. God only knows how I would feel if I didn't tell someone something I should have, and they pass away," I finished.

"I know how that is. I wish there were some things I could have told a few people. But no more living like that," Jared adjusted his jacket collar, "positive vibes only. That's why I'm being real with you right now," he added.

"I feel you, bro; but nothing will be positive about the news I have to give Jamie."

18

As I drove to the house, I tried my hardest to figure out how to tell Jamie about her uncle, but nothing came to mind. I pulled into the driveway and Jared put his hand on my shoulder.

We entered the home and Jacob came crawling to greet us.

"Hey, little guy," Jared spoke as he picked up Jacob.

I shook my hand in Jacob's hair and continued.

I proceeded to the kitchen to find Jamie and Madison laughing and talking.

"We're back," I mentioned.

Jamie got up and walked over to me and kissed me. "How did things go?"

The way she asked me this, reminded me of an innocent child asking their parents about their day.

"Baby, I think you should come with me," I told her before taking her hand.

Jamie displayed a concerned look on her face but allowed me to lead her.

I walked her to the bathroom and closed the door behind me.

"Daddy, what's wrong?" I could tell Jamie was getting nervous as her voice started to crack.

"Jamie, there's no easy way to put this," I started taking her hands into mine, "but it's about Michael. He's... he's dead," I finished.

Tears began to roll down her cheeks, as she turned away from me and put her hands over her face. I reached in to hold her and she jerked away.

"Baby, I'm sorry," I told her calmly.

"Why didn't you do anything?" she asked me.

"He was dead by the time we arrived, babe. There was nothing that any of us could do," I replied.

She wiped the few tears from her eyes.

"Do you all know who did this?"

I had to tell her the truth.

I adjusted myself and continued, "no. I have my suspicions, but I can't just completely say that the person is guilty unless I can place them at the crime scene."

"Who do you think is responsible?" she asked.

I released a sigh.

"I think Julie is responsible, Jamie."

Jamie raised her eyebrows.

"Are you handling this?" she asked.

I sighed again before speaking.

"No, I have chosen not to take this one," I confessed.

"Why? Is my family not important enough for you to handle cases like this?"

I could tell she was quickly getting upset.

"I guess you just want to go after my family to put them in prison; is that it? My family is all I have left and you're slowly eliminating them."

I could tell by now that the hurt Jamie was feeling, was quickly turning into anger.

"Jamie, calm down. That's not the reason, if I only went after your family to put them in prison, I would be taking this case." I softened my tone. "Come here," I told her.

"No, I don't think so," she folded her arms across her chest. "I think I need to be alone," she mentioned as she opened the bathroom door.

I put my hand on it and pushed it close.

"Jamie, don't do this," I told her. "You know that my intention is not to hurt you. I love you too much for that."

"Then why won't you take this case?" she asked me sternly.

More tears were welling in her eyes.

I honestly didn't have an answer.

The only thing I could make out of my mouth was, "I'm tired, Jamie. I want all of this to be done and over. I've been chasing after your aunt for many years now and it's a lot to deal with. Same old shit, just a different day."

Jamie was still hurt, and I could see the hurt in her eyes. She finally spoke, moments later.

"I'm going to open this door," she started, "and when I do, I suggest your hand not be on the frame."

I studied her face to see if she was bluffing at all. I saw no signs of it.

Rather than immediately move my hand, I surrendered and spoke in a passive-aggressive tone.

"You tell me what you want me to do and that's what I'll do," I spoke.

"Well first, I want you to move your hand from the frame. Then, I want you to leave me the hell alone and let me just think," she spoke, raising her tone.

I moved my hand and she jerked the door open.

She walked upstairs and slammed our door shut. I walked out of the bathroom to the kitchen, where Jared and Madison resided.

"Bro, you good?" Jared asked.

"I don't want to talk about it right now," I stated.

I walked out of the kitchen and walked upstairs.

"Jamie, open the door," I spoke as I knocked on the door.

As she opened the door, I looked her in the eyes. I could tell more tears had fallen.

Jamie held a suitcase in her right hand with some of her clothes and toiletries inside; just enough to go away for a short while.

"Where are you going to go?" I asked her.

"It's not because of the relationship, but I need time to think. I need to be left alone," she spoke, ignoring the question.

She walked past me and towards the stairs.

"Give me your bag," I told her. "I'll carry it for you," I submitted.

She passed me her suitcase and I walked it downstairs. She looked at me and hugged me.

"Madison, can I speak to you for a second?" Jamie called out.

Madison walked over and I walked into the kitchen.

"What just happened?" Jared asked.

"She's upset," I told him. "Which she does have every right to be. I just want for her to understand that my intentions aren't to hurt her."

"You're gonna have to elaborate a bit more, bro," Jared chuckled. "I mean, she's carrying a suitcase. Be real with me."

I slightly shrugged my shoulders.

"She's being extremely emotional right now. Which makes sense," I began, "she lost her cousin, had a shitload of shit go down yesterday; I feel her pain. She wants an escape," I finished.

"Damn man," Jared shook his head. "Whatever goes down, you know I got your back," he spoke. "It's hard on everyone right now."

Madison re-approached the kitchen after speaking with Jamie.

"Richard, Jamie's going to be staying with us for a short while," Madison spoke. "Is that okay with you?"

I looked at Jamie, who was crying silently.

"I don't mind if she stays with you all," I started. "Jamie's my heart, but if she needs to be alone, it's what she needs," I told Madison. "She just lost her cousin: a family member she was closest to."

"We'll make sure everything is okay with her," Madison spoke gently.

"Madison, baby, let's get ready to get out of here; I think Rick needs time to think," Jared suggested.

Madison hugged and kissed me on the cheek, before passing me Jacob.

I hugged Jacob tightly and passed him back to Madison. I shook hands with Jared before he picked up their bags.

Madison had Jacob in her arms and followed as Jamie left the home. Jared followed Madison, and I gently closed the door behind him.

My phone vibrated shortly after the four left. I glanced at the device and saw a text from Jamie had come through. I placed the phone in my pocket and closed the blinds. The sun was still shining, and so the room glowed a burnt red.

I decided to go upstairs and lie down. Once I was comfortable in my bed, I pulled out my phone and read the text message from Jamie.

Jamie: Ricky, I love you very much. I will be staying at Madison's home for a little bit, but I don't want you to think that I'm mad at you. I just need some time alone to think.

I placed the phone down without replying and closed my eyes.

***

A few months passed by, and Jamie was still staying with Jared and Madison. Michael's death took a toll on everyone, including the police force, and we hadn't punched any holes in the case.

I saw Jared as I was leaving the office.

"Yo, Jared! Hold on," I stated as I locked my door.

"What's going on?" he asked.

I caught up to him and shook his hand.

"How's Jamie?"

"Jamie's still the same Jamie that she was when she left," Jared started, "but things are going well. How have you been holding up?" he asked.

"I've been trying to make it, you know. Things have been hard since Jamie's leave and Michael's death has hit the force hard."

I thought about all of the protocols we had to follow and how we still hadn't had a break in the case.

My phone vibrated twice as Jared spoke. I noticed the message was from Jamie and I opened it.

"Who's that?" he asked as he saw a slight smile form across my face.

"It's Jamie. She says we need to talk," I told him. "I wonder what's up." I texted her back and she replied almost instantly.

Jamie: Tonight.

"Prepare for anything," Jared stated and shook my hand. "I gotta get going. Madison and Jacob are waiting on me for dinner," Jared stated.

"Alright, that's cool," I stated as we finished our handshake and walked to our vehicles.

"Let me know what happens tonight with Jamie," Jared spoke over the roof of his car.

"I got you," I responded.

I closed my door and Jared closed his. We both left the parking lot of the police station.

I went home, freshened up, and drove to *The House of Soul,* the place that Jamie wanted to meet. I walked inside and the greeter sat me at the same table that Jamie and I shared our first date.

Jamie entered the restaurant wearing a black trench coat.

I rose to my feet as she arrived at the table. I walked to the opposite end of the table and pulled the chair out for her to sit.

Before sitting, she hugged me, making sure there was distance between our bodies and she kissed me on the cheek.

"You look beautiful," I told her as I returned to my seat.

I stared at her curly, brown hair as she unzipped the coat slightly.

To me, Jamie seemed to be glowing and her skin was still soft to the touch.

"Thank you, Richard," Jamie started. "I called you here today, because I really wanted and needed to talk to you" she stated.

"What's wrong, Jamie?" I asked her.

I was curious as to why she hadn't taken off her coat.

"I missed you," she told me.

I raised my eyebrows, as I was a little shocked this came out of her mouth.

"Oh, you missed me?" I asked her.

I didn't doubt that she'd missed me; in fact, I missed her just as much, but I was just shocked this was the first thing from her mouth.

"Yeah, I did," she stated with tears forming.

"Jamie, not to argue or anything, but you told me to leave you alone," I reminded her.

"Yes, I did. I know, but babe, the time without speaking has made me miss you. It's made me realize what I have, or had."

Tears started to roll down her face and I wiped them.

"Jamie, look, I'm not an acquisition, you can't just decide when you want me in your life," I told her.

Part of me wanted to submit, but I really wanted answers from her. "Why is it that when I wanted to talk to you, you would constantly avoid it?"

"Because I was scared," she stated. "I was afraid that if I spoke to you, I would break down and just do something on impulse," Jamie added as her voice started to crack.

"So, I'm supposed to jump through hoops when you want to talk?" I asked.

The server approached our table.

"Good evening. How are you all doing this evening?" he asked as he placed the menus on the table.

"We're pretty good," I spoke.

Jamie reached over and held my hand.

"Can I start you all off with something to drink?"

"Yes, and thanks for asking. Can I have a glass of the Alizè? Make that 2," I corrected.

"No, I don't want that," Jamie spoke. "May I have a sprite, light ice?" Jamie asked.

"So, one glass of Alizè and one Sprite. I'll get that right out to you all." The waiter walked away and Jamie and I looked at each other.

"Rick, you didn't have to be here tonight, but you being here, speaks volumes," Jamie started again. "I know from the way I've been treating you, you probably just want to walk away and never hear from me again, but I have been so stressed."

I sat and listened to Jamie as she held my hand.

"Why didn't you just tell me what was wrong, Jamie? You left me without explanation and you gotta realize, I feel pain too," I spoke gently, yet firm enough to get the point across. "You're only thinking of yourself and what you want, but you try to make it as though I'm only thinking of myself. You're being stingy," I added.

"I can't do this," she stated and released my hand.

She rose to her feet and so did I.

"Why?" I asked. "Why can't you do this? Because it's the truth, Jamie? I've learned that when you say that, it's to avoid hearing the truth about yourself from a different viewpoint." I stated. "Now, sit down so that we can finish," I asserted.

Jamie rolled her eyes and sat down before I continued. She released a big sigh.

"If you don't feel like dealing with me, I understand."

"It's not even that, but I've been hurt before and I don't want to go back down that road," I informed. "You've been hurt, so why are you trying to act the way that others have acted towards you? I've tried my best to keep you on a pedestal Jamie, I even asked you to be my wife."

She looked at her hand and studied at the ring I put on her finger months earlier.

"And the fact that you still wear it, shows me that you want to be my wife. I still want to marry you, Jamie, but I do not like the way you've been treating me."

Jamie started to cry softly.

"I'm sorry," she responded.

I reached over and held her hand tightly.

"Look at me, Jamie."

She lifted her head and looked me in the eyes.

"I am in love with you, but this attitude and behavior have both got to go."

The waiter returned to our table with the drinks.

He placed the drinks down before asking if we were ready to order. I asked for more time and he walked away.

Jamie took a sip of her sprite and I offered her a sip of my wine.

"It's your favorite, isn't it?" I asked.

"Yes, it is," she began, "but I can't," she answered.

I looked at her inquisitively.

"You can't?" I asked her.

She unzipped the trench coat and took it off, revealing what was underneath.

"I'm three months, Ricky," Jamie told me with her hand over her stomach.

I was shocked, yet excited.

"Are you telling me..."

"Richard, you're going to be a father," Jamie stated. "And I don't want to do this alone," she added.

I rose to my feet and walked to her side of the table. She stood up and I hugged her tightly. She cried on my shoulder and I kissed her cheek.

"I've missed you so much, Daddy," she spoke.

"I've missed you too, Baby!" I added as a few tears flowed down my face.

We finished the embrace and I helped Jamie take a seat.

"You mean the world to me, Jamie. I want you to be in my life for the rest of my life," I told her.

She let out more tears and cried softly.

"What about your child?" she asked inquisitively.

"This is my word: I'm so happy that you're holding my seed. I would give a rib to be a part of my kid."

I held Jamie's hand tightly, as she seemed to glow more since she told me the exciting news.

We finished our meals at the restaurant and walked to my vehicle.

I opened her door and she climbed inside.

Jamie sat down and I closed the door behind her.

I walked around to my side and got inside of the car. I drove away from the restaurant and to my home.

When we walked inside, Jamie inhaled deeply.

"Home, sweet home," she chuckled.

She walked around the home, in an attempt to touch and feel everything as if it were her first time in the home.

I chuckled at Jamie before I took her hand and led her upstairs to the bedroom.

"It feels so good to be back," she squealed and flopped down on her back in the bed.

I couldn't help but laugh a little at this.

"Baby, I'll be back up in a minute," I spoke before walking downstairs.

I pulled out my phone and called Jared.

"Why the hell didn't you tell me?" I asked as soon as he answered.

"Congratulations man," Jared chuckled as he knew what I was referring to. "But you realize it's midnight," he chuckled.

"I know, but wake ya ass up," I chuckled. "We got shit to do. I want the wedding to happen soon."

"Well damn, I'm up now," he laughed. "What do you need?"

"You're my best man," I stated. "I want to help me make sure everything goes right, and I want to ensure the night is hers. I have a few connections at *Double X-L*, I'm gonna see if I can get some entertainment lined up."

"Who are you gonna get?" Jared asked.

"You'll see," I chuckled.

A few moments later, Jared and I hung up the phone.

I walked upstairs to bed and held Jamie close to me while placing my hands on her stomach.

"Goodnight, my bride," I stated to her. "Goodnight, little one," I added.

19

"It's your big day," Jared told me. "You nervous?"

Two months had passed since I'd found out that Jamie was pregnant, and she returned home. Finding out the information about her had me giddy on the inside and increased the amount of love that I felt for her.

"I've been waiting for this day, bro. But I guess I am a little nervous," I admitted as I felt the butterflies in my stomach. "Do you think something could go wrong?"

"It's your day. You have the force behind you. Don't worry about anything," Jared adjusted my bow-tie. "You just focus on making this the best day possible."

"You're right," I replied as I looked in the body mirror.

I was ecstatic. I was about to marry the woman of my dreams, who was also carrying my child.

But this also created a sense of panic, thus intensifying the tingling feeling that I was experiencing.

Jared and I exited the room and we saw the guests starting to enter the church: Madeline, Abel, Isabella, a few of Jamie's friends, and the band members and their instruments.

"Who's the band for?" Jared asked.

I never told him the entertainment that I'd reserved.

"Jared, I would like to introduce you to a friend of mine," I stated. "Ari Love."

Ari stepped into the room from the church.

"It's nice to meet you, Jared," she stated, and Jared extended his hand.

"My bro loves your music, Miss Love," Jared stated, shaking her hand.

"I hear you're a pretty big fan yourself," she stated. "And call me 'Ari'," she chuckled. "Miss Love is my mother."

"Yeah, I'm a fan," Jared spoke semi-excitedly. "It's just the good feeling of R&B and to know that some artists can still bring it."

"Well, I'll take that as a compliment," Ari chuckled. "Not too many guys are willing to say they're a fan of a female R&B singer."

"Gotta appreciate good music," Jared finished.

"I would love to keep chatting with you guys, but we've got a wedding to make happen," Ari smiled. "Jared, it was great meeting you," she spoke.

"The pleasure's all mine, Ari," he replied.

"Richard, I will see you soon," Ari shook my hand.

"Thanks, Ari."

Ari Love walked to the front of the church with the rest of the band members.

"So, that's who you were getting," Jared stated. "Must you keep everything a secret?" he joked as we both walked to the front of the building.

"Yeah, because your ass can't," I chuckled.

As the band finished setting up, my stomach felt as though it were doing summersaults.

"Breathe," Jared whispered as the band started to play music to fill the church.

The guests started to fill the seats of the room, and soon, the band played the introduction for the wedding.

Ari began to vocalize as the band played the instrumental.

The guests were all seated and Jamie entered the room with her godfather.

Ari started to sing her hit single, *Love in the Clouds*, as Jamie and her godfather slowly walked down the aisle.

"*I always knew that this would be, ohhh, the perfect love for me*

And God has blessed me in this way," she sang.

I was excited and nervous at the same time. The woman, who was once an accessory, now meant the world to me and was moments away from becoming my bride.

Jared put his hand on my shoulder to calm my nerves. On the opposite side of me, Jared, and a few more groomsmen, stood Madison and a few of Jamie's bridesmaids; tears filled their eyes.

Jamie was wearing a beautiful black and white dress and her baby bump was being displayed nicely through the dress, which brought more emotion to the church.

"*This love I have for you, it drives me crazy. Oh, no, never have I ever felt this way, but now I see.*

You're the one, I scream your name. You bring me joy, forget the pain,

Loving you, boy, takes it all away

It eases my mind and brings me joy. And it brings tears to my eyes," Ari started to hit high notes in her song and a few tears accumulated in her eyes.

"*Call her, Mrs. Young,*" she changed the lyrics to her song, "*I'm going to scream it loud. Because now, you're gonna keep your love in the clouds.*"

As the song ended, everyone rose and applauded as Jamie took my hand.

I shook hands with her godfather after she kissed him on the cheek and embraced him.

She took hold of my arm.

"We are gathered here today, to join these lovely two in holy matrimony," the pastor stated. "I've been informed that these couples have prepared their own vows and they want to keep things simple, so without further ado, the floor is yours," he stated to me.

I cleared my throat and spoke.

"Jamie, I love you with all of my heart and as I look at you today, I couldn't be more ecstatic. Ever since I first laid my eyes on you, I knew that there was something special," I looked her in the eyes.

Something about her stood out, as though she was glowing even more than usual. I continued to recite my vows to her.

"I've tried my hardest to be the man you wanted and you being here today, proves that you feel that I am. I love you with all my heart, Jamie, and I will travel to the ends of the Earth for you. I couldn't be happier as I stare into the eyes of the woman that I've fallen in love with, and to know that you are holding my child makes me even more emotional," I continued.

My voice started to crack and Jared put his hand on my shoulder. Jamie had tears in her eyes and reached into her pocket and pulled out a tissue. She wiped my eyes and I continued.

"I promise to love you, cherish you, and cause you no harm. I promise to always be the man you've fallen in love with and I pray that God allows us to live and see our little one grow older. I want to be there for the first words, first steps, first accident; and I want you to be my wife through it all. I am the man I am today, because of you. Jamie, I love you more than life itself," I finished my vows and the pastor spoke.

"That was beautiful," he spoke. "Jamie?"

"Richard, you're my best friend, my lover, my king, and in a few moments, you will be my husband. I can honestly say that since I met you, I have been in love with you. You're the man I've always dreamed of having; someone who's protective, loving, caring, and genuinely cares about me," Jamie inhaled sharply as she sniffled.

I smiled as she read the vows, and part of me wanted to lay a kiss upon her lips. I resisted temptation.

She continued reading her vows after wiping her eyes.
"You're the air that I breathe and you're the one I want to spend the rest of my life with. As I carry your seed, I can't help but hope that if it's a boy, he's just like you, or if it's a girl, you keep

her protected like you protect me. You're my king and I love you with all my heart."

Madison put her hand on Jamie's shoulder. The tears were moments away from running down her face.

"In a few moments, I will officially be Mrs. Richard Young and I couldn't be happier. We've had our share of ups and downs, but love conquers all. You make me smile and even when I'm at my worst, you manage to show me your best. Richard, I love you for this. You've made me a better woman, and I hope you can see that."

The church was in tears as Jamie finished stating her vows.

"Do you all have the rings?" The pastor asked.

Jamie turned to Madison, as I turned to Jared. They both gave us the rings and we turned back to face each other. Before we placed them on each other's hands, the pastor spoke again.

"Do you, Richard Young, take Jamie Perez, to be your lawfully wedded wife — for better or for worse, in sickness and in health, for richer or for poorer, 'til death do you part?"

"I do," I stated.

"And do you, Jamie Perez, take Richard Young to be your lawfully wedded husband— for better or for worse, in sickness and in health, for richer or for poorer, 'til death do you part?"

"I do," she stated.

"May I say something?" I asked him.

"You may," he stated.

"Jamie, with this ring, I want you to know that I'm symbolizing that I will love you when your hair turns gray; when it's 20 below in July; if you gain weight, it doesn't matter. As long as you remain the woman you are, I will forever love you."

Jamie started to cry tears of joy and the pastor continued.

"Well, what more can I possibly say after those words?" He added. "All I can say is 'by the power vested in me by the state of Illinois, I now pronounce you husband and wife. You may kiss the bride,'" he spoke.

I pulled Jamie closer to me and I proceeded to kiss her. As I retreated from the kiss, Jamie was smiling from ear to ear, and she was crying tears of joy. The audience rose to their feet in applause.

Ari's band started to play another song. I turned and gave Jared and the other groomsmen our signature handshakes, as pride filled my body.

"You did it, man," Jared spoke, excitedly.

Jamie turned and hugged Madison and the rest of her bridesmaids, as the tears flowed down her cheeks.

Members from the audience formed a line to congratulate Jamie and me.

Ari Love started to sing "The Only One" as Jamie and I shook hands with the congregation.

Julie stood at the end of the line to congratulate us, with a smirk on her face.

"How did Julie Wilson get in the building?" I heard Abel speak over his earpiece to the other officers in the church. "Watch closely for any sudden movements," Abel finished.

"Keep your cool," Jared whispered to me, although I could hear the tensity in his voice.

"Congratulations, Mrs. Young," Julie spoke as she clapped her hands.

Jared and Abel both approached and stood in front of Jamie and me. I held Jamie's hand tighter as I felt her tense up.

I tapped Jared's shoulder.

"It's cool," I whispered calmly.

He stepped to the side and I moved closer.

Jamie held my hand tighter and I spoke.

"Thank you, Julie," I stated and tried to walk past her, but Jamie wouldn't move.

I turned towards Jamie and spoke to her.

"Baby, this is our wedding day. I won't let Julie ruin this day for us," I uttered. "Right now, I need you to face your aunt. You're going to bear my seed and you're a Young now; don't let her interfere."

Jamie looked me in my eyes, and I could see the fear she possessed. Although she was frightened at Julie's presence, she submitted and agreed to proceed.

Ari Love noticed the commotion as she continued to sing. Julie went for a hug from Jamie while I held her hand.

As Jamie refused the hug, Julie put her hand inside of her jacket.

Immediately, Jared put his hands on his holster and Abel started to wave his hand towards Ari's bodyguards and a few of the other officers.

I immediately released Jamie's hand in case I would have to take Julie down.

"Woah," Julie stated with her hand still in her pocket.

"Take your hand out of your pocket Julie, slowly," I stated.

Julie looked at me sternly and finally spoke. "You don't trust me, do you?" She looked at me and noticed no sign of approval. "Good boy," she remarked as she moved her hand from her pocket.

"Boom!" she exclaimed to scare us. "I just wanted to give you all this card," she spoke as she showed us a card. She let it fall to the floor.

Julie raised her hand and flicked my chin.

As soon as her hand connected, I pushed Julie and threw a punch that didn't connect.

The congregation chattered and some members reacted negatively to me throwing a punch.

Jared grabbed me and held me, as Jamie quickly grabbed my hand and put it on her stomach.

Abel grabbed Julie and a few members from the audience approached us; it didn't take me long to identify them as some of Julie's bodyguards.

"How the hell did they get in here?!" Jared spoke aloud.

"Why don't we all just calm down?" Abel spoke as he held Julie.

Ari Love stopped singing and approached us.

"This is my wedding. I do not want Julie here," I spoke sternly. "I better not see you at the reception," I spoke.
"Baby, you feel that. Calm down... please. The baby doesn't like it," Jamie spoke as the baby started to move around inside of her.

I slowly turned around and hugged Jamie tightly, as more tears began to roll down her face.
"Ms. Wilson, we're going to need to ask you to leave," Ari spoke from behind us as she approached the front. "My friend, Richard, doesn't wish to have your presence."
"Ah, so you're Ari Love. You work with Kai-G and B. Smoove, right?" Julie asked. "Don't worry, I was just leaving," she continued. "Sorry for wanting to wish my niece the best on her wedding day," Julie retorted.
Julie slowly turned around and exited the building with her bodyguards.

I held Jamie and I could feel the baby begin to kick.
I kneeled to her stomach.
"Don't worry little one, Daddy's okay," I spoke to Jamie's stomach and Jamie told me that the baby stopped kicking upon hearing my voice.
I kissed her stomach and rose to my feet.

The remaining audience members applauded and Ari picked up the microphone.

"I want to thank everyone for taking the time out to be here today, on behalf of the bride and groom as well as King Pin Entertainment," she announced. "If you would like to see more of this lovely couple and spend more time with them, there will be a reception at their home immediately following this wedding. Thank you all for coming," she spoke.
"Ari, I want to thank you for your help," I told Ari as she lowered the microphone and the band began to pack up. "Listen, we may not need for you to sing or anything, but we would be honored if you could attend the reception," I told her.

"I would need to check my schedule," Ari mentioned. "I may be needed back at the studio," she admitted.

"Well, if you're able to, we would love for you to be there," I rebutted. "But Ari, this is my bride, Mrs. Jamie Young. Jamie, say hello to one of your favorite R&B singers, Ari Love," I spoke.

Jamie was speechless and she reached out her hand.

"I'm a hugger," Ari chuckled as she motioned for Jamie to approach her.

I released Jamie's hand; she and Ari embraced.

"I can't believe that you're here at my wedding," Jamie spoke with excitement. "Babe, you're the best," she smiled at me.

"I'm going to call Kaiden and see what's going on back at *The Base,* that's what we call the studio, and I'll let you know for certain."

"If he can, invite him along as well," I suggested.

"I will do that," Ari spoke as she stepped away for the moment.

"You have made this perfect," Jamie spoke seconds after Ari walked away.

"Anything to make you smile, baby," I assured her.

Jamie opened her arms for an embrace, and I picked her up off of her feet.

I laid a kiss upon her lips and Ari walked back over.

"Yall are too cute," she chuckled. "And girl, that baby bump is everything," Ari put her hand on Jamie's stomach.

"Thank you," Jamie smiled.

"No problem," Ari replied. "So, great news. Kaiden said things are cool back at King Pin. So, I'm free to attend your reception. He and Byron are also going to try to make an appearance."

"That's love," I responded. "Thanks, Ari."

"Well, let's hop to it," she chuckled. "Let's get this party started," Ari replied as the band members walked to the front of the church.

Jamie and I walked down the steps, and people were on both sides of us, still congratulating us. We both entered the limousine and the chauffeur drove off.

"So, baby, how does it feel to be Mrs. Richard Young?" I asked Jamie.

"Come here," she whispered to me.

As I moved closer to her, she put my hands on her stomach.

She gave me a passionate kiss, which seemed to be never-ending. As I touched her stomach, she put her hands on my leg and slowly rubbed my thigh.

"Maybe we should calm down because if not, you're going to have twins, Mami," I joked with her.

She bit her lip, seductively. Her hormones were raging, but she agreed that we should stop.

"I love being Mrs. Young. You're my world, babe."

"I love having you as my woman and my wife. I'm looking forward to spending the rest of our lives together," I added.

The limousine was soon approaching our home and we entered the backyard for our reception. As we entered the reception, everyone was excited to see us and immediately started to cheer.

As we celebrated, I couldn't have been happier that Jamie was now my wife and our future looked bright.
***

20

"Daddy, I'm so happy right now," Jamie stated as we lied down in bed.

I wrapped my arms around her as she rested on my chest.

"You've made me the happiest guy alive Jamie," I told her as I kissed her forehead.

Two months had passed since the wedding and we were patiently awaiting the arrival of our angel.

We'd found out the gender and babyproofed the house.

We'd packed boxes of clothes to make room for the baby, and we had them stacked neatly near our bedroom door. A crib sat in the corner of the room, as well as a lounge chair.

In an instant, however, our joy was interrupted as the door to our room came flying open.

Three men, all dressed in black came running in with guns aimed. "Don't move!" the men shouted.

Jamie held on to me tightly, but I immediately sat up and pressed the emergency button near the bed to alert Abel and the rest of the team that we needed assistance and to come with no lights or sirens.

I'd thought of the idea to put buttons that would silently call the police stations around the home, if Jamie was home alone and needed assistance, she'd be able to quickly get help.

Julie entered the room behind the men and I pulled my gun out from under my pillow but hid it in my pants.

"Jamie Young. It's cute," she stated as she chuckled. "Still want to try me, Ricky?" Julie asked.

Jamie started to cry as she held her stomach.

I kissed Jamie on the forehead, as I rose. "Jamie, come on baby," I mentioned to her.

I helped Jamie to her feet; Julie was disgusted at the sight of Jamie's stomach.

"Where do you all think you're going?" Julie asked.

I didn't reply verbally. I just glared at Julie and continued to walk with Jamie towards the washroom.

"Oh really?" she questioned. "Do it," Julie instructed one of the men and he shot me in the shoulder.

"Fuck!" I shouted as Jamie screamed.

"Ricky!" Jamie screamed as she grabbed my arm.

"Baby, go back to the bed!" I demanded as I sat on the floor holding my wound.

"I'm not leaving you right here," she stated to me, even though I was less than 100 feet away from the bed.

"Baby," I held my wound, "do not jeopardize yourself or our little girl. Please, I will be okay. It's just a flesh wound."

Anger filled my body, and I remembered I had my weapon, but I was outnumbered. I didn't want to jeopardize Jamie or our daughter.

Jamie walked to the bed while holding her hand over her mouth. Julie threw a towel my way and told me to put it over my wound.

"We don't need you bleeding out too soon, do we?" Julie was smiling deviously.

She enjoyed the feeling of power; a feeling she hadn't felt in a while since the police were hot on her trail.

I spit in her direction.

"Fuck you, Julie," I told her while holding my arm.

As her company aimed their guns at me, she motioned for them to lower them.

"Gentlemen, please exit the home. I would like some time alone with my niece and nephew-in-law," Julie stated.

The three men all walked past me with their guns lowered and exited my home.

Once they left, I rose to my feet.

I looked at Jamie and saw the tears in her eyes. I held my shoulder as I walked over to the bed.

"Did I ask you to move?" Julie asked me. "Why the fuck do you insist on defying me?"

I didn't share any words with her, but Jamie eyed her aunt up and down.

"Now, we're going to do things my way. I ask questions and you all answer them accordingly. Consider this my trial, where we already know I will win," Julie continued.

Jamie rested her head on my chest and cried silently.

"When did you two first get together?" Julie asked.

Neither Jamie nor I answered, and Julie pulled out a gun.

She aimed the gun at me.

"I believe I asked you all a question."

I tapped Jamie so that she knew I wanted to readjust. She lifted her head and I moved my body, so I could sit up and the headboard would support my back.

"You remember when you sent her on the first mission? The one where she was arrested?" I asked Julie.

Julie didn't reply; she stared at me.

"That was when we first met," I answered.

"Ricky," she shook her head and chuckled. "Are we working with criminals to solve a case, or are you just fucking them for your own satisfaction?" she suggested.

I continued to hold my shoulder while staring at Julie.

Jamie kept her head on me.

"Question two: was it always the plan to try to catch me, Rick? Were you using my beautiful niece from the very beginning?" Julie eyed Jamie. "Well, she isn't beautiful anymore; she's no more than your hoe."

"I would appreciate it if you changed the way you refer to my wife," I asserted.

"Baby, just be quiet," Jamie pleaded.

Jamie knew how her aunt's attitude was when she got upset. She knew exactly what Julie was capable of, and for my safety, she wanted me to let Julie talk.

"Shut up hoe," Julie retaliated. "You turn your back on family for a man who isn't worth shit. Look at you now, eight months pregnant and you can't do shit."

"At least I got married and I have a family. I have someone who genuinely loves me and cares about me; something that you still haven't shown me. Everything you've told me has been a lie," Jamie mentioned while holding my hand tighter.

I could tell the baby was kicking.

"Julie, listen," I stood. "You've picked the wrong day to come and try to take over some shit," I mentioned as I got closer to her face.

I could tell Jamie feared for me and herself, but I was more focused on getting Julie out of the house. So, whether it could be accomplished through playing mind games or antagonizing her, that's what I was going to do that.

"Fuck you," Julie stated.

"I should have kicked your ass two months ago when I had the chance," I told her.

She slapped me while holding the gun.

"Shut the hell up," she stated.

After she slapped me, I lost my temper.

I grabbed Julie and tackled her to the ground.

She lost control of her gun and it flew out of her hand. She punched me in my wounded arm and tried to crawl for her gun.

"Get your ass back here," I shouted as I pulled her back towards me; the adrenaline was rushing through my body.

I dropped my elbow into her leg as she pushed me back on the ground. I punched her in the face and we continued to struggle as she was trying her best to reach her gun.

"Jamie, secure the bag!" I shouted to Jamie as Julie and I struggled on the floor.

Jamie reached in the dresser beside the bed and pulled out a gun and shot once.

The bullet hit Julie in her arm and she punched me. Julie hit me in my wounded arm and shoved me. I fell backward into the stack of boxes.

"You little bitch," Julie spoke as she picked up her gun and put it in her back pocket.

The gunshot didn't seem to have any effect on her.

She pulled out a pocket knife and approached Jamie while holding her arm. Jamie tried to shoot again, but no bullets remained in the gun. Julie slapped Jamie and the impact caused her to lay on the bed.

Julie showed the knife to Jamie and smirked.

I knew I had to act quickly. I adjusted my body and tied a tourniquet around my arm using the towel on the floor.

"I will be taking my niece today and will be leaving," Julie spoke.

She lifted Jamie's gown to reveal her stomach and Jamie started to cry.

Julie straddled Jamie so that Jamie couldn't move her legs. She kept her knees on Jamie's joint where the elbows connected, so that she couldn't move her arms.

She made the knife touch Jamie's stomach.

Jamie screamed, and I pulled out my gun.

Julie rolled one of the small sheets into a ball and forced it into Jamie's mouth.

"I can't deal with all this screaming," Julie spoke.

She picked the knife up and quickly looked back at me to check and see what I was doing.

I planned to shoot her in the back of the head, but once I saw her turn around, I took the shot.

I shot three times; one bullet hit Julie in the forehead, one entered directly into her left eye, and the final in her chest. Julie fell to the ground and dropped her knife; Jamie cried harder.

I was too weak to stand, but I heard someone running up the stairs.
I aimed my gun and almost fired the weapon.

"Woah, hold your fire bro," Jared stated.
I was relieved to see him; even if it was a second too late to deescalate the situation.

He entered the room and helped me to my feet.
Jamie was in shock, and she couldn't move. All she could do was cry.

As I stood, he ran over to Jamie to take the balled-up sheet out of her mouth and as he removed the sheet, he stepped on Julie's body; she still had both eyes open although one had a bullet inside of it.

"Oh shit," he stated out of shock as he pulled out his gun and almost shot at Julie.
I'd walked over to Jamie and was now hugging her.
"She's dead, Jared," I spoke.

It was finally over, and although she was still shaken up, I knew Jamie was proud it was over as well.

He put two fingers to her neck; no pulse.
"Are you all okay?" he asked.
Jamie couldn't say anything, she was still terrified; I held her tighter.
"Luckily, I was the only one injured," I joked with Jared. "It's a flesh wound."
Jared looked at my tourniquet.
"Aw damn," he chuckled, "you really need that for that baby wound?"

I rolled my eyes at him and I let out a sigh of relief.

"Can you believe this bitch tried to cut Jamie and take the baby out of her?" I asked him.

Jamie buried her face in me. She still couldn't believe what had just transpired.

I put my hand on her stomach and felt the baby moving and kicking.

"Little one, Daddy's right here. Shh," I whispered. "Mommy and I are fine," I mentioned.

"Is she really dead Jared?" Jamie finally spoke while still hugging me and resting her head on my chest.

"She's beyond dead Jamie," Jared spoke.

Abel and two other officers came upstairs and noticed the blood around the room.

Jared walked to the bathroom and got the first-aid kit to cover my wound.

"Jamie, look at me," I stated.

As she looked up, I saw the tears in her eyes and I spoke again.

"You were amazing, baby."

"No, I wasn't. Otherwise, I wouldn't have allowed it to go so far," Jamie added while looking at my wound.

"You froze, which is a normal human reaction, but you came back once I gave you direction. That's courage, Mami," I kissed her on the cheek. "This is a mere flesh wound, ignore it. We are all safe, but we probably wouldn't be if you hadn't taken charge," I told her.

Jamie felt slight satisfaction knowing that I was proud of the actions she took.

"I love you," she stated.

"I love you more than you'll ever know," I told her.

I looked up and noticed the other officers in the room.

"Get me some cars over here at Young's residence," Abel stated as he walked over towards Jamie and myself.

He looked down at Julie's body and back up at Jamie and me.

"Are you all okay?" he asked.

"Just shaken up a bit," I admitted to him. "But we're fine."

"I see what happened to her and I have an idea as to why it happened; not to mention we've detained three men in front."

"Go on and charge them," I spoke. "They were here with this piece of shit," I looked at Julie's body.

"Guys, let's move into another room," Abel suggested. "When the crime techs get here, we don't want to have anything disturbed. We want for the evidence to line up exactly how we tell them it went down."

I helped Jamie to her feet, being careful not to disturb Julie's body. We all walked into the adjacent room, and we had a seat on the bed.

"Okay. Young, I need for you to tell me exactly what happened," Abel spoke as we sat.

Jared came from the washroom and began to apply the patch to my wound.

I told him exactly what happened, starting with the men entering the room.

Once I finished telling Abel what happened, he shook his head.

"Honestly, I'm more relieved that you and this beautiful woman are okay," he mentioned. "I just needed for you to tell me so that I can defend you. I can't do that if I don't know."

"That's love, Roberts," I spoke as I shook his hand.

Madison came walking up the stairs next and walked over to hug Jamie and me.

"Oh my God, are you all okay?" Madison asked as Jacob crawled on the bed to Jamie.

Jamie lifted the infant, as I spoke.

"Everything's okay. She's gone now," I referred to Julie.

Madison hugged us once again.

"I'm so glad you two are safe."

"Nothing's going to happen to us, not if I have something to say about it," I spoke.

Jacob reached over to me and I let him sit on my lap.

"Jacob, I never told you. This is your aunt Jamie, and this is your cousin," I stated pointing to Jamie's stomach.

Jamie fainted and fell back on the bed.

"Jamie!" I shouted.

Everyone seemed to jump up as Jamie passed out on the bed and Madison took Jacob from me.

"Where are those cars?!" Abel shouted over his radio.

I put my hand over her heart and still felt a beat, but the beat was very faint.

Jared gave me his jacket to put around Jamie's shoulders.

Paramedics entered the room a few seconds later with a stretcher. They lifted Julie's body onto it and while they walked Julie's body downstairs, Jared and Abel picked up Jamie's body and were frantically moving to get her to the ambulance.

A paramedic reached out and took her. He laid Jamie on the gurney in the back of the ambulance.

"I'm riding with her," I stated. "I'm her husband."

"How far along is she?" the female medic asked me.

"She's about eight-and-a-half months," I stated. "Why, what's wrong?" I held her hand.

"Her water just broke," she answered.

Madeline was the next to arrive on the scene, and she got information from Jared as to what was going on.

I called to Jared as they prepared to close the ambulance doors.

"Jared, lock up the house for me and drive my car to the hospital," I mentioned as I tossed him my keys.

"What about the crime scene?" an officer asked.

"Put tape on that bitch, it will have to wait," Jared shouted.

I shook Jared's hand and they closed the door to the ambulance.

The ambulance drove off and I gripped her hand tighter. Paramedics were shouting words across and putting an IV and fluid into Jamie's arm.

"Will these medicines harm the baby?" I asked, skeptical of what they were putting into her body.

"Sir, to be honest, we're trying to save the baby. Her blood pressure's sky-high and we need to lower it," he mentioned.

"Jamie, can you hear me?" I asked her. "If you can, squeeze my hand." I felt a slight squeeze to my hand and I continued to speak to her.

"Baby, they are trying to save you and our angel; I need you to stay with me, Mami."

Jamie slightly opened her eyes and moved my hand to her stomach. The baby was kicking and moving around. I kissed her stomach as the baby continued to jerk around.

"My little angel, Daddy and Mommy need you to calm down," I spoke. The baby stopped moving as much but continued to kick on occasion.

I held Jamie's hand tightly as the ambulance arrived at the hospital. They wheeled her into the delivery room and had me put on sanitized scrubs over my clothes.

"Last recorded blood pressure was 165 over 100," a nurse called out.

"How long ago was that taken?" another nurse spoke.

"About five minutes ago."

"Let's prepare to deliver this baby," the lead nurse spoke.

"Jamie, it's time to push," I told her as they prepared.

They prepared for a C-section and I interrupted the process

"Stop! I can communicate with her. She's going to push," I told them.

I could tell they were skeptical, but then the doctor spoke.

"Husband's orders. Do it his way."

"Come on Jamie," I spoke to her. "Baby, I need you to push," I said speedily. "Little one, it's time," I mentioned to the baby.

Jamie pushed about five times before the baby was born, and it took another few seconds before the baby breathed on her own.

I kissed Jamie on the forehead and the doctors walked away with my daughter.

"Where's my baby?" Jamie asked softly.

"We're just taking vitals and cleaning her up," a nurse responded. "She's about a month and a half early, so we have to double-check and make sure she's breathing okay and can function on her own."

I kissed Jamie on her cheek and held her hand.

The doctor brought the baby back to us swaddled in a blanket.

"Good news, she's healthy enough to leave here in a few days with you all," he spoke.

Jamie held the newborn in her arms.
"Our precious little girl," she spoke to me.
She looked at me and I kissed her on the lips.

"She has your eyes," she stated.
"Yeah, but look at all this hair," I joked while touching the baby's hair. "This is yours. And look at her nose and mouth: also, yours. I think you made her by yourself," I chuckled.
"Richard, we have a precious little girl now and I know we will raise her right," Jamie said.

"After all that you and I have been through Jamie, I'd say she is a blessing; maybe even a miracle," I remarked with a smile.
"Miracle!" Jamie exclaimed. "That's going to be her name; what do you think?"
"Let's find out." I motioned for the baby and Jamie passed the newborn to me.
I picked her up and the baby used her hand to hold my finger and appeared to smile at me; I knew that she knew who I was by the tone of my voice.

"You are Daddy's little Miracle," I stated to her.
The baby smiled and squeezed my finger even more.
"I think she likes it," Jamie stated with a smile.
"Miracle Yvonne Young," I stated proudly.
"I love it," Jamie squealed as the nurse wrote the name on the clipboard.

I held Miracle in my arms as I walked over to the window where Jared, Madeline, Madison, and Abel stood.

"Miracle, look," I stated while holding her to the window. "That's your Uncle Jared, your Aunt Madison, Madeline, and Abel."

I paused and looked at Jacob.

He was standing on the window sill with his hands against the glass.

"And that," I stated pointing to Jacob, "that's going to be your best friend, someone to look over you when I'm not able to: Little Jacob," I spoke.

I saw Madison, Jared, Madeline, and Abel give signs of approval, as Jacob kept his hand on the glass.

I walked back over to Jamie with Miracle. I passed the baby to Jamie.

"That's right," I spoke, "she's our little Miracle."
***